on the road

#1

LEAVING HOME

Stephanie Doyon

Aladdin Paperbacks

First Aladdin Paperbacks edition May 1999

Text copyright © 1999 by Stephanie Doyon

Aladdin Paperbacks
An imprint of Simon & Schuster
Children's Publishing Division
1230 Avenue of the Americas
New York, NY 10020

Typography by Steve Scott
The text for this book was set in Wilke Roman.
Printed and bound in the United States of America
10   9   8   7   6   5   4   3   2   1

Library of Congress Cataloging-in-Publication Data
Doyon, Stephanie.
Leaving home / by Stephanie Doyon. —
1st Aladdin Paperbacks ed.
p.   cm. — (On the road ; #1)
Summary: When eighteen-year-old Miranda decides to postpone
college and travel across America instead, she encounters difficult
situations which require self-reliance and independent thinking.
ISBN 0-689-82107-7 (pbk.)
[1. Self-reliance—Fiction. 2. Voyages and travels—Fiction.]
I. Title. II. Series: Doyon, Stephanie. On the road ; #1.
PZ7.D7783Le   1999
[Fic]—dc21   98-44736
CIP   AC

In loving memory of
Raymond Bernier

We've barely made it out of the driveway and already I'm wondering if I'm about to make the biggest mistake of my life. Doubts are munching at my insides, telling me not to go through with it. Why now? Why wasn't I this scared three weeks ago, when I still had a chance to back out?

As soon as we hit the first stop sign, my father leans across the front seat and mumbles something to my mother that I can't quite make out from the back. Mom nods in her silent, mom-like way and says nothing. A thin film of sweat dampens my palms. *Can they sense I'm having second thoughts?* There's nothing they'd like better than to have me chicken out. I'm sure of it. I bet their offer to drive me to New York isn't a peace offering at all, but really just a big plot to get me to ax my plans with Kirsten. Am I paranoid? Maybe. But you don't know my parents. They're two very intelligent, very persuasive people who don't give up easily. I should've seen this coming.

"We're just going to make one quick stop—okay, Miranda?" Mom says, relaying the message from the passenger's seat. The worry lines in her forehead are deeper than usual, spreading out over her eyebrows like a map of the Connecticut highway system. As a concerned mother and active member of the Yale Alumni Association, she's pretty upset with me for deciding not to go to college right away. My dad, the stern-looking guy sitting behind the steering wheel, is a third-generation Yale graduate. He's hardly spoken to me in a week, using Mom as his interpreter instead. It was getting so bad, our house was starting to feel like the United Nations.

My eyes blur as we zip alongside the low stone wall that hugs the curves of Stanwich Road. "Okay," I answer easily, even though my tightly wound insides are dying for an explanation. What's so important that it has to be taken care of *before* they drop me off at Kirsten's apartment? Why can't it wait?

"What'd you do with your portable CD player?" my younger sister, Abigail, asks. She's been so quiet until now that I've nearly forgotten she's sitting right next to me. "You're not taking it, are you?" she asks, showing me her braces with one of her quirky fourteen-year-old grins.

"There's no room." I slide my big blue backpack off my lap and place it on the seat between the two of us. "I packed it away in my closet."

2

Abigail fiddles with the pack's various nylon straps and zippered pouches, pretending, I think, that she's the one who's leaving and not me. "It seems like kind of a waste to leave it in the closet for so long . . . don't you think?"

I turn my head back toward the window, pretending not to get the hint. "Think what?"

"It's a waste."

"What's a waste?" As a big sister, I figure it's my duty to be difficult on occasion, if for no other reason than to teach Abby that things don't always come easy in life. Besides, if I didn't give her a hard time, she'd always be borrowing my stuff.

Abigail lets out a deep, dramatic sigh, obviously trying to decide how much trouble my CD player is worth to her. "Leaving the CD player in the closet while you're gone," she answers heavily. "Isn't it a waste?"

"No," I say, upon giving her question several moments of serious consideration, "I don't think it's a waste at all."

After fiddling with her light brown French braid in frustration for a few minutes, Abigail finally gets up the courage to ask me straight. "Do you think I could borrow it? At least until you get back?"

The flicker of hope lighting my sister's green eyes is achingly familiar, reminding me of how I'd begged my brother, Jayson, to borrow his mountain bike when he left for Yale last year. "You'd better not break it," I warn.

3

"Promise." Abigail smiles in sweet relief, touching my backpack again. "This trip is going to be so cool, Miranda. You're going to have tons more fun than if you were just hanging around here. This summer is going to be *so* boring."

Boring is highly underrated. At least when things are boring, you know what you're getting—safety, comfort, and no nasty surprises, I think nervously to myself as I wipe my sweaty hands on the legs of my jeans. *I'd give anything to be bored right now.*

Does anybody need anything?" Dad says as he rolls into an empty parking space in downtown Greenwich, right in front of Robert's Pharmacy. So *this* is the super-secret destination they were whispering about?

"I'd like a soda," Abigail chirps. "Root beer, if they have it."

Dad glances over his shoulder, but looks out the back window instead of at me. "Miranda?" he booms.

Hearing my father talk directly to me without Mom having to intervene is enough to make me jump out of my skin. "No thanks," I answer back, bracing myself for whatever stealthy plan he's about to put into motion. The car door slams shut, and I carefully watch the back of Dad's salt-and-pepper head as he disappears into the pharmacy.

What's he up to?

"He just wants to get a newspaper," Mom explains, once again proving my suspicions that a) she can read my mind, and b) she's a terrible liar.

Yeah, right. There are so many things wrong with what Mom just said, I don't even know where to start. First of all, we get the paper delivered to our house seven days a week, so there's no reason in the world why he'd have to stop now to buy one—unless our goldfish ate the financial section, which seems pretty unlikely. Second, it's no coincidence that we're parked next to Beans & Books, a bookstore café that *coincidentally* just happens to be one of my favorite places *on Earth*. Dad probably figures I'll get all weepy, break down, and won't be able to leave. As a backup plan I wouldn't be surprised if he had the entire Yale faculty gathered nearby, just waiting to descend upon the car like a swarm of honeybees, stinging me mercilessly with college statistics until I beg to be enrolled in the fall semester.

"I just have to ask you this one more time, then I promise I won't ask again." Mom flips down the visor and looks in the mirror, pretending to smooth a few wisps of her brown bangs, but our eyes meet in the reflection. "Are you sure this is what you really want?"

"Come on, Mom, we've been over this a billion times. . . ." The rebellious reflexes are kicking in automatically, making my mouth answer instead of my heart. I hate the way I sound— all crabby and overconfident—but I can't seem to help myself. "Why would I go if I didn't want to?"

"I know," she answers softly. "I just thought I'd ask."

Glancing out the window, my throat is raw with guilt for snapping at my mother on my last day at home. *My last day at home.* Suddenly, the thought of taking a trip across the U.S. makes my head feel heavy and tired. All I really want to do right now is curl up somewhere safe and familiar, like in one of those great purple overstuffed chairs at Beans & Books.

Mom reaches back for my hand and lets out a long sigh. "I don't want you to feel like you have to prove anything, Miranda. If you get out there and realize it's too much for you, you can come home. We can have you enrolled at Yale for the spring semester."

Frowning, I slink back in my seat. On my list of the Top 100 Things I Want to Do at This Point in My Life, going to college is pretty close to the bottom, ranked somewhere between #89 *Shoveling compost for a living* and #97 *Contracting a flesh-eating bacteria.* When are my parents going to realize that college isn't for everyone, and that it may not be right for me? My friend, Kirsten Greene, the one I'm going to be traveling with, is a prime example of someone who didn't go to college but who is doing perfectly well. Being a bike messenger isn't exactly Mom and Dad's definition of success, but Kirsten is able to take care of herself and she's pretty happy. What more could a person want?

"Or if you don't want to go to school right away, that's fine, too," Mom says, reading my mind again. "The point is we'll always be here for you—no matter what." She gives my hand a warm squeeze and turns quickly toward the front again, but not before I catch a glimpse of her damp eyelashes. "I'm really proud of you, honey. You're so strong and determined—I wish I had had the courage to do what you're doing when I was your age. I know you're practically an adult now and can take care of yourself, but I'm a mother—I'm still going to worry."

The stinging rawness in my throat sharpens. *I'm a fraud*, I tell myself. *A fake.* These past few weeks I've spent every ounce of energy trying to convince everyone that I'm an adult who's capable of making adult decisions, and now that I have at least Mom's approval, I feel like I've misrepresented myself. I'm not as brave or as strong as she says I am. The truth is, I'm terrified of what's out there. And I'm not taking this trip because it's something I feel extremely passionate about—it's just that I'm not thrilled with the other options.

"You have to send us tons of postcards," Abigail says, interrupting my thoughts. On her lap is the travel journal Jayson gave me as a going-away present, and she's flipping through the clean, blank pages begging to be filled with stories. "And you have to take lots of notes so I'll know where to go when it's my turn."

"Oh, no, not you, too." Mom exhales tiredly. "My nerves are going to be completely shot by the time the two of you finally settle down."

Dad returns to the car and, to my surprise, he's alone. Wordlessly, he hands a soda to Abigail and then he drops a small paper bag in my lap. I lift a stunned finger to trace the border of the blue logo printed on the bag. BEANS & BOOKS. I can't believe it. He must've gone in when I wasn't looking.

Abigail nudges my elbow and nods at the bag as if to say, *What is it?*

I shrug, then reach in and pull out a slim yellow paperback. *The Backpacker's Manual: A Guide to Touring the United States.* For a brief instant my heart stops beating. Dad isn't going to hold me back anymore—he's letting me go.

A painful lump hardens in the middle of my throat, and the toes of my hiking boots involuntarily tap an erratic, panicky beat against the floor mat. Part of me is relieved by Dad's silent blessing—after weeks of arguing and then hardly talking at all, I didn't want to leave feeling angry. At the same time, there's this weird emptiness tunneling through my chest like I've just been abandoned. Why isn't he trying harder to make me stay?

"It's supposed to be a pretty good guide," Dad says as he backs the car out of the parking space.

"The woman in the travel section said it was the best one they had."

"It's great, Dad—thanks." While I struggle to fit the book into the crammed front pocket of my pack, we drive away; the road leading us away from downtown, away from Greenwich, away from Connecticut, away from the only life I've really ever known. Every once in a while I catch my father stealing worried glances at me in the rearview mirror. I pretend not to notice, gazing silently out the window at the passing trees and smiling confidently, as if I know exactly what I'm doing.

The truth is, I really don't have a clue.

This isn't the first time I've been to New York City, but it might as well be. I go into Manhattan several times a year with my family because my dad works in the Wall Street area, at the southern tip of the island. His investment firm is in one of the World Trade Center Towers, on the eighty-fifth floor, and from the boardroom you can look down on the Statue of Liberty, across the Hudson River, all the way into New Jersey. It's amazing how peaceful the city looks from above. We go to Midtown, too, to go shopping at the Fifth Avenue stores at Christmastime, take in a musical in Times Square, or have dinner in one of the great restaurants overlooking Central Park. You know, all the glamorous, New York things you read about. It's great and everything, but it's all a little too perfect for my taste. I'd rather see the grittier side of New York with all the dirt and chaos. Perfection gets stale after a while.

"What street does Kirsten live on?" Dad calls over his shoulder, suddenly slamming on the brakes to avoid a yellow cab that cuts right in front of us on the West Side Highway. In a chain reaction, the driver of the beat-up delivery truck right behind us slams on *his* brakes, his rusty radiator grille coming within inches of our back bumper. The driver sticks his face out his open window, shaking his fist and yelling something I'd rather not repeat.

"Tenth Street between First and Avenue A," I read from my notes. "She said we should take the Fourteenth Street exit. . . . "

"Is that it?" Abigail asks, pointing to the exit sign as we are about to drive right past it. Dad clenches the steering wheel and turns a hard left.

"Mitchell!" Mom screams as Dad tears the car across three lanes of traffic to make the exit. Horns honk and tires squeal. I wait for the seemingly inevitable crunch of buckling metal and broken glass.

"Hold on!" I wheeze. My pack skids across the back seat and squishes Abigail against the door. "Sorry . . . "

Abigail clamps down hard on her lower lip as if she's trying to stop herself from laughing out loud. "Welcome to New York," she giggles under her breath. I wish I could laugh, too, but I'm too busy squeezing my eyes shut, praying we make it through the intersection without being crushed to smithereens.

When all four tires land safely on the pavement,

I open my eyes. The blood quickens in my veins as I take a look around Fourteenth Street, the wide, four-lane thoroughfare that Kirsten told me forms the northern border of Greenwich Village. We drive by huge meatpacking warehouses with men loading crates into the backs of refrigerated delivery trucks. Further east, the long city blocks hold a seemingly endless stream of open-air discount stores, the merchants perched on high metal stools right on the sidewalk selling windup toys, luggage, perfume, and New York City T-shirts in every color and size. There's a man carving mangoes into flowers with a pocketknife. People are everywhere—walking dogs, drinking bottled water underneath storefront awnings, zooming in and out of traffic on in-line skates, buying pretzels and hot dogs from street vendors, waiting on the corners of each block for the traffic lights to change. So many things are going on at once, so many different lives are intersecting and separating. The whole scene pulses with a kind of energy and movement you just can't find in Connecticut. Or probably anywhere else.

At Second Avenue, we turn and head south toward Tenth Street. "Her apartment should be pretty close," I say, the excitement building as I count down each block. *So this is the East Village, the neighborhood Kirsten told me so much about* . . . . The streets are crawling with the young, the hip, and the unconventional, lending to the area's bohemian atmosphere. Kirsten said a lot of struggling artists and musicians live in this part of the city, which is why it's so cool and funky.

Judging by the frightened look on my mother's face as we drive by The Second Avenue Body-Piercing Parlor, I'd say she had a few different adjectives to describe the East Village.

"I don't know about this place," she says, her voice heavy with apprehension. "It looks a little *seedy*."

"Mom, please . . . Kirsten's been living here for almost two years. She says it's fine." Personally, it looks *great* to me—in three short blocks I've already spotted two discount bookstores, a vintage clothing store, and a tiny little café I'm dying to check out. I absolutely can't wait to go exploring.

"You won't go out by yourself, will you?" Mom asks.

Abigail rolls her eyes in sympathy.

"I might," I answer honestly. There's no point in lying. "It depends on what Kirsten's doing."

Dad glares at me in the rearview mirror. "You're not going out by yourself at night," he orders, joining the worry-fest. "It's not safe."

It's hard to imagine why I would go out by myself at night, but there are always unforeseen things that can happen, and I'm a firm believer in not making a promise if there's a chance I can't keep it. "I *probably* won't go out alone," I answer

14

firmly. "But you never know what might happen."

"There is no reason why you should be out alone. Period," he says forcefully.

How does he do it? I marvel to myself. *I'm eighteen years old, but he still makes me feel like I'm five.*

"All right, Dad," I relent, hoping it will satisfy him enough to get off my back. "I'll make sure someone's with me if I go out."

You'd think my answer would be enough to appease him, but he just keeps going. "We can't be here to guide you, Miranda—you have to take responsibility for yourself. Every action has a consequence, and part of being an adult means analyzing the possible consequences *before* you take action. . . . "

Blah, blah, blah . . . How many times have I heard this speech before? Three hundred million times? By the way my parents carry on, you'd think I was a problem child who was always getting into trouble. Just once I wish I had the courage to stop Dad in the middle of one of his rants and say, *Look, I've always been one of the most rational, responsible teenagers out there. You don't have to give me speeches. I may not be as perfect as Jayson, but I'm still a good kid.*

But, like always, I say nothing.

I think that's Kirsten's apartment building over there," I say, pointing to the narrow gray five-story walk-up across the street with the numbers 357 painted in bold black on the glass window above the green entrance door.

Dad's jaw tenses, and Mom's shoulders sag a little. It's a cool building with lots of character, but I'm sure the only thing my parents notice are the crumbling facade and the iron bars on the windows.

"It's only for a few days," I say. "Until Kirsten gets everything squared away." No one says another word for what feels like a full five minutes—the only sound that can be heard is the idling of the engine. I'm not quite sure what to do next. My spine melts into the seat. What's everyone waiting for?

The suffocating silence and the dread of our impending good-bye are even more oppressive than the hot, restless itch that's seeping deep into my muscles. For the moment, the nagging doubts have faded into the background, overshadowed by a resurgence of the intense curiosity that made me take this trip in the first place. The world is waiting for me just beyond the car door, but somehow it seems impossibly far.

I reach for my pack with one hand and touch the door handle with the other. "Uh, I guess I'm going to go now. . . . " I clear my throat and wait for someone to move or talk or just do *something*. Abigail leans over as if to give me a hug but is suddenly thrown back into the seat when Dad unexpectedly stomps the gas and zooms into a parking space about twenty feet away. The air eases out of my lungs in a long, drawn-out sigh. *Why is he acting so weird?*

"We're going in with you," Dad says, cutting the engine.

No, no, no, no! The screaming in my head is so loud, you'd think they'd be able to hear it.

"You don't have to," I plead as delicately as possible, "I'll be fine—really."

Mom gives her mauve lipstick a final touch-up. "Miranda, you can't expect us to drive all the way here and just drop you off. I want to meet this Kirsten person."

"You mean you want to grill her. . . . " I mumble to myself.

"What was that?"

"Nothing," I sigh.

One by one we pile out of the car: Mom and

Dad wearing their most concerned parental expressions, Abigail as happy as a clam to tag along, and me stifling a dreaded groan with each step. You might think that having my family meet Kirsten is no big deal, but I'm not so sure it's going to end there. I have visions of my family huddled together like a bumbling tour group, trailing five feet behind us all the way across America. *"You really don't have to follow us anymore, Mom,"* I'd say once we crossed the Mississippi River. *"We'll be fine."* Then Mom would touch up her lipstick and say, *"Miranda, you can't expect us to follow you all the way out here and just turn around. . . . I want to see the Rockies."*

"She lives on the fifth floor, and there's no elevator," I say, making one last-ditch effort to change their minds, but no one listens to me. What's Kirsten going to say when she opens the door and sees the four of us standing there like a bunch of fools? What am I going to say? Has a reasonably healthy teenage girl ever sustained traumatic injury from severe embarrassment? Would I be the first?

Taking a deep breath, I press the buzzer and look down at the ground, searching for a hole to crawl into.

Miranda! It's so great to see you!" Kirsten shouts, throwing her arms around me the second she opens the door. "I can't believe you're here!"

"I can't believe it either . . . ," I stammer, struggling to think of something interesting to say. It doesn't help that Mom, Dad, and Abigail are waiting out in the hallway, ready to pounce.

Kirsten looks so different than I remember—her shiny black hair has grown out from the boyish pixie she had in school and is now almost down to her shoulders, framing her oval face. She looks so happy and so pretty—totally grown up. Her clear, slate-blue eyes hold me in their steady, self-assured gaze.

"You look great," I can't help but say.

"So do you," Kirsten answers, touching one of my long curls. "Your hair is still as red as a fire engine. I was thinking of dyeing my hair your color, but I didn't want people on the road thinking we were twins."

19

We look at each other and laugh and hug again. To look at us, you'd think we were best friends who were reunited after living apart for many years. The funny thing is, we hardly know each other at all.

"*Ahem*—" Dad crashes the party with his not-so-subtle throat noises.

Kirsten wrinkles her straight nose. "Is someone in the hall?"

"Yeah . . . " I shrug sheepishly and step inside the doorway, my stomach clenching in a mortified lump. "My mom and dad and sister, Abigail, wanted to come in and say hi. . . . "

Ugh. So this is what total and complete humiliation feels like. *Just shoot me now and put me out of my misery.*

Kirsten pops her head into the hall. "I'm sorry—I didn't realize you were standing out there. . . . Please, come in," she apologizes, ushering everyone into her apartment and shaking hands with them as they walk through the door. "I'm Kirsten Greene—it's such a pleasure to meet you."

I'm floored by her coolness.

"Nice to meet you, too, Kirsten," Mom says as we all try to squeeze into the dark, windowless kitchen. Abigail is suddenly seized by a fit of shyness and ducks behind my father's tall frame, causing me to back up a couple of feet and unwittingly bump into Mom with my pack. I turn just in time to see the thinly veiled look of horror in Mom's eyes as she gets pressed perilously close to a sink heaping with dirty dishes.

"Can I get anyone some herbal tea?" Kirsten offers.

"No thank you," Dad grumbles.

"We just had brunch. . . . " Mom's hands flutter nervously around her throat.

Abigail just stares at the floor.

Thanks for trying to act normal, guys—I really appreciate it.

"Well *I'll* have some tea," I say, slipping the pack off my shoulders and leaning it against the fridge, eager to disassociate myself from my weirdo family.

Kirsten opens the cupboard. "Phew—that was a close one! It's a good thing only Miranda wanted tea, because I have only one clean mug left!"

My parents exchange disapproving glances, and I get caught in the cross fire, their scrutinizing eyes boring into me with laser-beam precision. *So what if she doesn't like to spend her whole day washing dishes?* I argue silently. *Why make a federal case out of it?*

Kirsten pops a mug of water into the microwave. "Sorry there's not a lot of room in here for you to sit down," she apologizes, motioning to the retro chrome kitchen table and chair set. Every available seat is littered with an opened stereo

21

console that looks like it's been dropped off a fire escape. "My roommate actually thinks that hunk of junk can be salvaged. What an optimist."

"Oh?" Mom grasps for a thread of conversation. "What's her name?"

"Who?"

"Your roommate . . ."

I was sort of hoping this wouldn't come up.

Kirsten doesn't even blink. "*His* name is Vance," she says in a way that makes me think she must have the two most modern, understanding parents in the world.

Unfortunately, mine are not.

Oh, boy, I cringe, *strike two.* One more, and I'll be on my way back to Connecticut faster than you can say "house arrest." Gritting my teeth, I await the avalanche of questions that are about to come tumbling our way.

Dad parts his puckering lips as if he wants to say something but can't quite formulate the most tactful combination of words. For a second there it looks like he might have something, when, thankfully, his train of thought is blown to bits by the beeping microwave.

I love microwaves.

"Let me give you guys the grand tour. . . . " Kirsten hands me the fragrant cup of hot tea, then gracefully waves her arms in the air like a real estate agent showing a million-dollar property. "This apartment used to be one huge room, if you can believe it," she says proudly. "We converted it ourselves."

"Who?" Dad asks, the corners of his mouth scrunching wryly. "You and *Vance?*"

Mom elbows Dad in the ribs. I take a fast, nervous sip of the hot tea and burn my tongue. My eyes water as Kirsten points toward a pair of white louver doors covered with grimy fingerprints.

"That's Vance's room. Believe me, you *don't* want to see what's in *there*. . . ."

I bury my face in the cup and burn my tongue all over again. When she thinks no one's looking, Abigail presses an intrigued eye against the dark crack in the door.

"My room's over here," Kirsten says, leading us toward a matching set of louvers on the other side of the kitchen. The opened doors reveal a surprisingly tidy, nicely decorated room with a few plants and a lot of sunlight. There's barely room for more furniture than the twin-sized bed and small bureau that are already occupying it, but the high ceiling and a couple of brightly colored throw pillows give the room a light, comfortable feel. I could be totally happy living in a room like this.

"Your plants look very healthy," Mom says, nodding toward some sprawling green thing that's in a hanging pot. "You must take good care of them."

Kirsten shoves her hands boyishly in the back pockets of her black jeans and nods. "A friend of mine gave me the spider plant, and it was practically gone—she kills just about every plant she touches. It took me a few months, but I got it back. I wish I didn't have to leave them behind, though. Vance won't take care of them."

"It's a lot of work, but very rewarding," Mom says, the lines on her forehead fading a little. "I grow roses and a few herbs and vegetables."

An enthusiastic grin crosses Kirsten's face. "That's one of my dreams—to have a garden of my own someday."

Mom ventures a timid smile. "You'll have to stop by and visit us in Connecticut so I can show you ours."

"I'd love it."

My mom and Kirsten are actually having a conversation. The gigantic knots in my stomach unravel slightly as we shuffle out of Kirsten's tiny bedroom. *Who would've thought?*

Maybe this won't be such a disaster after all.

Kirsten's living room is an odd sliver of space left over from the two constructed bedrooms, so narrow that we practically have to walk single file to get in. Mom, Abigail, and I squeeze together on the futon that will be my bed for the next few days. It's covered with this furry leopard print that's so awesome, it gives me the chills. Dad takes a seat on one of two clear vinyl inflatable chairs, like the kind you'd see in a dollhouse but a thousand times bigger. He squirms a little, trying to get comfortable, the vinyl squeaking with every move. The metal industrial table lamps, the plastic pillows—it's all so . . . *New York*.

"Where's Jayson?" Kirsten asks, draping herself across the other vinyl chair. "I was kind of hoping to see my old chem lab partner."

"He's spending the summer in Virginia building houses," I say, setting my mug down on the homemade coffee table, its top a wild collage of glossy magazine cutouts and random stickers.

Kirsten arches her sleek black eyebrows. "Mr.

Finance Major is working construction? A year of college can really change a person, can't it?"

"Jayson hasn't given up finance," Dad clarifies. I notice his face turning an irritated shade of pink. "He's just doing a little volunteer work this summer. The organization he's working for builds low-cost housing for needy families."

Kirsten's face lights with recognition. "Is it Habitat For Humanity?"

Dad nods sternly, the vinyl chair squeaking in agreement.

"I can see Jay doing that—he's always been such a nice guy," Kirsten gushes. "Maybe Miranda and I should go visit him on our way through."

The redness in my dad's face subsides.

"Now there's an idea. . . . " Mom pats my knee. "He'll be there until the end of August. That'll give you plenty of time to visit."

I don't answer either way, because like I said, I don't like to promise something and not be able to follow up on it. Even still, my parents are all happy again, and the tension suddenly drains out of the room like water from a bathtub. Just the idea of having my responsible older brother keeping an eye on me for a while seems to make all the difference in the world to them. It doesn't exactly thrill me.

"Do you think you'll go to Virginia right away?" Dad looks directly at me when he says this, his eyes showing none of the anger and hurt he's been clinging to these last few weeks. I'm his daughter again.

I clear my throat and approach the subject carefully, not wanting to spark a new confrontation. "I don't know . . . we're not sure," I answer in a wimpy, vague voice. "We haven't decided where we're heading first—have we, Kirsten?"

"It doesn't matter to me," Kirsten says, shrugging. "I'm up for anything. I just want to get to the Southwest at some point."

"Oh, Miranda, you absolutely have to see the Grand Canyon!" Mom says with a sudden, awe-inspired burst. "I've always wanted to go there."

"And you should try to get up to Yellowstone," Dad adds, sinking so far into the vinyl chair, his knees are almost up to his ears. "It's enormous. You could literally spend weeks there."

"The Rockies are beautiful, too," Mom says. "And the Great Lakes."

Dad nods. "Try to see New Orleans and Chicago if you happen to end up near either one. And even though it's far, San Francisco has always been my favorite city."

"I'd go to Hollywood," Abigail says almost inaudibly.

My head is spinning. It seems like it could take years to see everything.

"I plan on visiting San Francisco once Chloe's settled there," I say, my stomach fluttering like a hummingbird's wings. "I want to see everything I can—but Kirsten's seen a lot of the country already."

A shadow falls across my mother's face. "How do your parents feel about you leaving, Kirsten?"

Kirsten's jaw grows rigid. "My dad couldn't care less," she says, her voice as sharp as a steel blade. "And my mom doesn't even know."

The conversation evaporates into the atmosphere, and we're all silent, absorbed in our own individual bubbles of thought. This is the point where, if we were visiting relatives on a Sunday afternoon, my dad would predictably smack his palms on his knees and say, *"Shall we?"* to my mother, who would say, *"Yes, we really should be going. We don't want to keep you any longer—I'm sure you have things to do."* But this is Saturday, not Sunday, and we're at Kirsten's apartment in New York, not at some relative's house in Connecticut, and I don't know when I'm going to see my parents again. I can't predict what they're going to do at all. I'm just praying they keep it short and sweet and don't get sloppy on me. I'll die if they make a scene.

My eyes do a loop around the room about five times, but no one moves. Finally, Dad heaves a long sigh, slaps his knees, and stands up. "Shall we?"

On cue, Mom jumps to her feet. "We really

should be going. I'm sure you girls have a lot to do before you leave. . . . "

I can't believe it! They used their worst line on me—their own daughter! I'm totally appalled. . . .

"It was great meeting all of you," Kirsten says as we all shuffle back to the kitchen.

"It was nice meeting you, too," Mom and Dad answer in unison.

Kirsten shakes their hands again. "We'll be very careful," she says, slipping back into the living room to leave us alone in the kitchen. "You don't have to worry."

With arms dangling limply at my sides, every part of my body feels weighted down. I know what's coming now and I'm tired. I just want the moment to be over.

So this is it—the big Good-Bye.

Leaving home for the first time is something you look forward to almost from the time you're born, and you think that when your moment comes there will be some secret, mystical ceremony that takes place—a wave of a magic wand and *poof* . . . you're an adult. The reality, though, is how quietly the moment slips by, so quiet that it kind of makes me wonder if maybe I missed it. Nothing has changed, and yet everything has changed, all at the same time.

"Have a great year in school, Abby," I say, giving my sister a bear hug. I'm really going to miss her. "Show them who's boss in field hockey."

"I will," Abigail says, squeezing me tight. "I'm going to miss you. You'd better send me post-cards—I want tons of them!"

A hot wave creeps up from my throat to my cheeks. I open my mouth to make a wisecrack, but my voice won't cooperate.

Mom rushes toward me with liquid eyes and outstretched arms. "My baby's leaving the nest," she coos, kissing me on both cheeks. Her face is damp. "I'm going to miss our chats. Promise you'll call us often and let us know how you're doing— I'll never get any sleep otherwise."

"I will," I squeak painfully. Although my eyes are burning hot, they're still dry, but not without a struggle. *Come on, keep it together*, I scold myself, biting the insides of my cheeks. *It's almost over.*

Dad places his hands on my shoulders. "I'll buy you a car if you don't go through with this. . . . "

"*Dad. . . .*"

"Just kidding." He kisses my forehead and rests his chin lightly on the top of my head. "Be safe, okay? We want you to come back to us in one piece. All right?"

I nod but I don't look him in the eye because I know I'll fall apart.

"I love you, Pumpkin," he says.

"I love you, too, Dad."

He pulls away from me, but I can still feel the weight of his hands pressing down. "Now go out there and get this travel bug out of your system."

He says it like it's a disease. Why can't he just wish me luck, instead? I watch them walk out the door and down the stairs and I keep watching long after they're out of sight.

I guess this means I'm on my own now—just like I always wanted. I stand in the doorway, hugging myself, my lower lip trembling no matter how hard I try to stop it. They were here just a second ago, driving me nuts, and now—there's all this empty space. *You know, maybe I'm not ready for this after all. . . .*

"They left, huh?" Kirsten says, tiptoeing back into the kitchen.

I start to say something to show Kirsten how cool and in control I am, but seconds later my heart cracks wide open and I start blubbering like a baby. "I'm sorry . . . ," I whimper, my face stinging with humiliation. "I feel so stupid."

"It's okay, Miranda—" Kirsten hands me a paper towel and puts her arm around me. "There's nothing wrong with being close to your family. I wish I was close to mine."

I've been in the bathroom for ten minutes and I'm in no hurry to leave.

"Are you all right in there?" Kirsten says, knocking on the door. She sounds concerned, but I don't know her well enough to be able to tell if she really cares or if she's just plain annoyed.

"Yeah, I'm okay—" I mumble, staring back at my blotchy red cheeks and green, bloodshot eyes that look like Christmas. Despite countless splashes of cold water and a few breaths of fresh air from the tiny window above the toilet, my face just won't calm down and get back to normal. This has always been one of my biggest curses—fair, sensitive skin that betrays every emotion, sometimes even before I feel it and usually long after it's gone.

"Do you need anything?" Kirsten asks.

"No."

I know she's wondering if hooking up with me was such a good idea after all, and really, who could blame her. You'd think I've never been away from home before. What a baby.

"Do you want a glass of water or something?" she asks.

"I've got plenty of water in here, thanks." I flush the toilet so she can't hear me sobbing.

"I hate to take off on you, Miranda, but my boss called—he wants me to deliver a few packages this afternoon. He's short on messengers today. The jerk's holding my last paycheck, so I guess I'd better show up." There's a long pause. "Are you going to be all right?"

"Sure—I'll be fine." I turn away from the mirror and lean against the old, rust-stained porcelain sink.

"I'm leaving the keys to the apartment, in case you want to go out. The square key is for the building, the round key is for the apartment, and the short key is for the dead bolt. Got it?"

"Yeah, I think so," I say to the door.

"I'm also leaving you a few subway tokens and a city map, in case you need it."

I press a wad of tissues the size of a baseball to my runny nose. "Thanks."

"And you have my phone number, right? Just in case?"

I start to laugh, but it comes out more like a hiccup. "I'll be fine, Kirsten, really. Go to work."

"Okay—I'll be back around seven or so . . . have fun!"

When I hear the front door latch close and I'm sure Kirsten's not coming back for anything, I head straight for the freezer to fill a washcloth with a few ice cubes for my puffy face. The ice looks old and dusty, and the tray is cracked, but it works for me. Even with the old ice, the dirty dishes, and the stereo parts strewn all over the kitchen table, I can see why Kirsten likes it here. It doesn't have to be a palace—it's just nice to have a place to call your own.

My best friend, Chloe Bartlett, has a completely different idea about things. She's a ballerina and she wants to be rich—I mean *really* rich—and famous. Chloe doesn't believe in settling for anything less than the best when it comes to just about everything, even if she really can't afford it. Like when we were shopping for prom shoes and she spotted a designer pair for $195 she just *had* to own. The day before we'd seen a pretty good knock-off at the mall for around $30. I would've sprung for the cheapies, but Chloe wouldn't dream of buying them, even though she was probably going to wear the shoes only once. She ended up putting the expensive pair on layaway and, even though she gets a pretty hefty allowance from her dad's child support checks, it still took her six weeks to pay off. Chloe says the only way to become rich and powerful is to act like you already *are* rich and powerful. Maybe she's right, but I still don't see how an expensive pair of shoes is going to change your life all that much.

I press the ice pack to my face, feeling instant relief as the blood vessels in my cheeks start cooling down. It makes me laugh to think if Chloe could see me standing in Kirsten's kitchen right now. Her pretty heart-shaped face would be warped by a mixture of shock and mild disgust, just like the face she'd made when I'd told her I'd decided to go cross-country with Kirsten.

"Kirsten Greene? Are you nuts?" Chloe had shouted in the women's dressing room at Bloomingdale's, her appalled face and Calvin Klein price tag reflecting back at me infinitely in the three-way mirror. "Tell me this is a joke."

"I couldn't be more serious," I said, slinging my legs over the arm of the overstuffed leather waiting chair, my usual post. "Why would I make it up?"

"What about Yale?"

"I can go next year," I argued. "What's the rush? I've got my whole life ahead of me, right?"

"I suppose," Chloe answered primly, turning from side to side to get the full effect of the chocolate-brown shift she was trying on. "But, *Kirsten?* Why do you want to go with someone who's so . . . "

"So what?"

Chloe huffed her blond bangs in the air as if the answer was obvious. "I don't know . . . she just seems a little rough around the edges."

I didn't like the way the conversation was heading, but I was hardly surprised. Ever since

Chloe had been accepted into the advanced dance program at the San Francisco Ballet, she'd turned into a colossal snob. If we had just met, I seriously doubt we would've become friends at all. But when you've hung around with someone since third grade, it's hard to blow her off, even when she's being a jerk.

"Kirsten's great. You don't even know anything about her," I snapped.

"Neither do you," Chloe answered coolly. "Come on, Miranda. The girl was a loner in school. Now she could be an illegal arms dealer for all we know."

"Cut it out, Chloe." My eyes made a quick scan under each dressing room door for eavesdroppers. "Kirsten's parents got divorced when she was little, and her mom moved a lot after that, dragging Kirsten around with her, which is probably why she was afraid to get close to people. I'd think you'd be more understanding, considering you know what it's like to go through a divorce."

Chloe's doelike arms reached effortlessly behind her back to unzip the dress. "And she wears the same pair of ripped jeans practically every day," she added with disdain, apparently not listening to a word I'd said. "What's up with that?"

Glancing down at my knee jutting from a big hole in my own jeans, I hardly felt as if I was in a position to criticize. "Who cares what she *wears?* This is a great chance for me to do something different with my life. I'm sick of Connecticut—everyone's the same here. I'm ready to meet new people and try new things."

"Fine—but do you have to do it with her?" Chloe wriggled out of the brown dress and tried on a silky black one. "Don't you think it's a little strange that this girl—whom you barely know, by the way—calls you out of the blue to go traveling with her? If you ask me, she's using you."

"Using me for what?" I bounded irritably out of my seat. The rows of cubicles and the fluorescent lights were making me feel claustrophobic. "Kirsten needs a travel buddy—why is it so shocking that she'd ask me? When we sat next to each other in study hall, we'd talk about traveling all the time. Is it *that* surprising that someone wants to be friends with me besides you?"

"I didn't mean it like that," Chloe said, shaking her head. "I'm not trying to crash your party, but it wouldn't hurt you to open your eyes and see what's going on. You're too trusting of people sometimes."

"Maybe I'd rather wait for someone to give me a reason not to trust them instead of automatically being suspicious," I answered.

"Look, I'm just saying I've dealt with Kirsten's type before," Chloe warned. "Believe me—she'll take whatever she can get."

You couldn't be more wrong, Chloe, I think to myself as I dump the leftover ice into the dirty spaghetti pot sitting on the counter in Kirsten's kitchen. Admittedly, Chloe's harsh words did cross my mind a bunch of times on the ride over here, but as soon as I saw Kirsten, I knew Chloe's accusations were way off base. I'm an excellent judge of character, and I can tell you there's no way Kirsten would use me—at least not deliberately, anyway. Chloe doesn't know what she's talking about.

I snag the keys Kirsten left me and the subway tokens, the map, and my detachable day-pack and head out of the apartment. Skipping down flight after flight of stairs, I can't help but think of Chloe and Kirsten and Yale and my family—and how my life's been going so far. It's funny how almost nothing turns out the way you planned.

When the light changes, I cross First Avenue in front of a virtual army of yellow cabs, lined up threateningly like tanks ready for battle. The air on the street is thick and hot, rising up from the pavement and licking at the soles of my boots, already making me wish I'd put on my cooler sport sandals instead. It must be at least ten degrees hotter here than it was at home. The concrete and steel buildings seem to trap the sizzling heat like a mammoth oven.

Okay, this is definitely weird. . . . I look straight down the middle of the avenue and see towering buildings in the distance stacking up like dominos for miles until they seem to dissolve in a haze of exhaust fumes. All of a sudden, I get this strange sensation like the air's being slowly squeezed out of my lungs and my body feels limp and I'm afraid to move. The buildings seem to be sliding further and further away from me, like looking through the wrong end of a telescope.

I'm alone. Completely, totally, unbelievably alone.

In New York City.

Maybe it's not a big deal to people who are used to hanging out in big cities, but this isn't the sort of thing that happens every day to someone like me. The whole thing is . . . well, intimidating.

What if I get lost and can't find my way back?

What if I pass out on the street and hit my head against the sidewalk and no one helps me?

What if I get kidnapped and my captors throw me in a dark, smelly basement with rats and gigantic cockroaches, never to be heard from again?

All right—I'm getting a bit carried away. But you get the idea. When I was little and my family went on vacation, whenever we spent the night in an unfamiliar city I'd get really freaked out. It would start with this odd tingling sensation in the pit of my stomach, and pretty soon I was convinced that at any moment the world would tilt at a ninety-degree angle and we'd all go sliding off the edge. I must've thought our home was the center of the entire universe, the only place where gravity worked and nothing bad could ever happen. Everywhere else seemed strange, unpredictable, and dangerous.

Now that I'm on unfamiliar turf again, that long-forgotten tingling is once more simmering in my belly. The traffic signal changes to green, and the yellow tanks roar past just as my foot reaches the curb. The quickening of my pulse cuts through the foggy cloud of anxiety. *This is New York,* I remind myself. *Things move fast. There's no time to be nervous.*

On the corner, a Hispanic man in his early twenties wearing a white T-shirt and a black backpack is holding a Day-Glo pink flyer in his hand. "Storewide clearance . . . VCRs, air conditioners, everything's got to go!! One more flyer to give away and I can go home!" he shouts to anyone who'll listen. Two girls about Abigail's age walk by eating soft ice-cream cones, ignoring the bright pink piece of paper thrust right under their upturned noses.

"Thank you, ladies," the man calls to them in a friendly voice, bowing in their direction. "Enjoy your ice cream!"

Several people pass by the man without a second glance, as if he were invisible. It's amazing that people can do that—just pretend that someone isn't there. Are city people as cold and unfriendly as they look? Or are they just sick of people handing them flyers on every street corner?

"One more to go!" he shouts again. "Help me out . . . someone?"

A young mother pushing a baby carriage directly in front of me curves around the man in a wide arc so her toddler's grabby little fingers stay at a safe distance. The baby gurgles something to the man and smiles, while the mother pushes ahead forcefully, her eyes staring straight ahead. No one seems willing to help the guy out. I feel bad for him. It's starting to look like he just might have to spend the rest of the afternoon in the sweltering heat.

"Here comes a nice person," the man says, waving the pink paper in front of my face. "Help a guy out, won't you? It's my last one. . . . "

Without losing a step, I give the guy a half-smile and take the flyer from him. I want to be nice, but not *too* nice. Then he'd think I was a tourist.

The man grins broadly and points to me. "See this, everybody?" he shouts into the air, "Take a good look at this woman—the only nice person in New York!"

Even though I'm trying to keep a straight face, I keep wrestling with an embarrassed grin that's determined to make an appearance. It feels pretty good doing something nice for someone else.

With his last flyer gone, I thought the man would start heading for home, but instead he reaches into the backpack and pulls out another flyer from his secret stash. My flyer wasn't the last one at all. Far from it. He has at least another fifty in there.

"One more to go," the man says, winking at me before resuming his sales pitch. "Who else feels like being nice?"

I spot a trash can a few feet ahead heaping with crumpled-up hot pink flyers that dozens of other "nice people" have thrown away. Oh, well. A grumbling noise suddenly erupts from my stomach like an earthquake, reminding me with urgency that I haven't really eaten anything all day. Mom and Dad took us out for pancakes, but I was so nervous, I only had a few nibbles off Abigail's plate.

Luckily, every other doorway on the block is a restaurant, which should make it pretty easy to find something. There's a vegetarian burrito place, but I'm not in the mood for Mexican. A few doors down I spot an Italian bistro—it looks expensive. Then there's a Jewish lunch counter proclaiming to have the best chopped liver in the city. Sounds tempting. *Not.* I finally settle on a small, clean deli with buckets of colorful fresh-cut flowers for sale outside the doorway. It looks cheap and fast.

There is so much food to choose from, it's unimaginable that it all can fit inside such a small store. Most of the floor space in the deli is taken up by two stainless-steel buffets, one with cold salads and pretty sushi rolls, and the other with trays of hot foods like fried chicken and pork lo mein. It all looks so good, but in the end I opt for the portability and economy of a bagel. I pick out a big, puffy one covered with poppy seeds.

"Cream cheese?" a chubby guy with thick glasses asks from behind the counter.

"Just a little," I say. He nods, then scoops a fist-sized blob of cream cheese and smears it on my bagel like he's spackling a wall with cement. If this is a little bit of cream cheese, I'd hate to see what he considers to be a lot.

44

While the deli guy wraps up my bagel in waxed paper, I read the pink flyer that for some odd reason I haven't bothered to throw away yet. WIZARD ELECTRONICS—STOREWIDE BANKRUPTCY! The bold black letters scream. EVERYTHING MUST GO TO PAY CREDITORS! UNBELIEVABLE PRICES! Underneath that is a list of boring appliances I couldn't imagine ever wanting to buy, but at the very bottom of the page there's something that catches my eye: LOCATED DIRECTLY ACROSS THE STREET FROM THE STRAND BOOKSTORE.

"Have you ever been to this place?" I ask the gray-haired woman behind the cash register, showing her the flyer.

She peers at the bottom of the flyer, then shakes her head. "Sorry," she says, giving me my change.

Outside, I take half the bagel and wrap the rest of it in the waxed paper, tucking it safely away in my day-pack for later. Biting into the bagel's crisp and chewy crust, I can feel the poppy seeds crunching between my teeth. A light wind rustles the sparse trees planted in the sidewalk, and I breathe in deeply the complex mixture of pungent and earthy street smells. The weepiness is starting to fade away, and already it's beginning to feel like my parents dropped me off days ago. I don't know what's going to happen in a few days when we're on the road, but for now I'm on my own with a good bagel and a bookstore address. Things are looking up.

45

Excuse me, miss."

A middle-aged man in a charcoal business suit clears his throat a few times. When I don't move he gives up, deciding to walk around me instead.

People start streaming by me in all directions, bottlenecking into the single door at the entrance of The Strand. A woman lets out a loud, aggravated sigh. "Some people," she mutters just loud enough for me to hear.

"Sorry . . . ," I murmur as I get swept up in the flow of the crowd. I didn't *mean* to block the doorway, it's just that when I saw the red-and-white sign that says EIGHT MILES OF BOOKS I freaked. Eight miles! All of a sudden I can't remember my own name, let alone the names of my favorite writers. Where do I start?

Moving through the turnstile, past the large security guard in the maroon blazer, I feel an instant burst of adrenaline pulsing through my system. This place is just crawling with discount books. Stark tables are piled high, and every shelf is jammed. Loaded cardboard boxes block the aisles. Unlike the cozy, library feel of Beans & Books, The Strand is a plain, wide-open room with a chipped linoleum floor and spray-painted, stenciled signs marking each of the categories. There are no comfy chairs or fancy displays. It's just books, books, and more books.

Wandering through the narrow maze of twenty-foot-high industrial-metal bookshelves, I'm dwarfed by the volumes of fiction towering above. Slowly, favorite writers and books come to mind as they appear before me: *To Kill a Mockingbird*, Harper Lee. *The Diary of Anne Frank. The Grapes of Wrath*, John Steinbeck. *The Catcher in the Rye*, J. D. Salinger. *The Collected Stories of Flannery O'Connor.* Every book comes in all kinds of editions—hardcover, pocket-sized, paperback; some with plain covers, others with beautiful illustrations. It breaks my heart that I can't buy them all.

While I'm totally submerged in book heaven, a gorgeous guy with curly blond hair, a striped T-shirt, and a beaded choker suddenly appears in the aisle next to me with an aluminum stepladder and a cart of random books. I grin to myself. Who cares if I just spotted a mint-condition first edition of *The Catcher in the Rye*? I'm sorry, but this is *so* much more interesting.

I try to look casual, stealing glances out of the corner of my eye. The red name tag pinned to the guy's chest says RICK. Good solid name, but unfortunately not a boyfriend name. Boyfriend names should always be two syllables or more so they can linger sweetly when you say them—*Stev-en, Mich-ael, Joe-y*. The longer the name, the sweeter it sounds. *Nich-o-las. An-ton-i-o.* Am I right? One-syllable names, on the other hand, snap—they belong to guys you'll probably just end up being friends with. The quicker you can say a guy's name, the less time there is for him to get the wrong idea.

I guess I could always call him *Rick-y*.

While I ponder what to call this beautiful boy, the shelving unit towering over our heads is swaying. It's only moving a few inches on either side, but just enough to make my heart jump. Rick's angelic face shows no sign of alarm as he scales the ladder higher and higher with an armful of books.

He's not going to put more books up there, is he? It's a miracle the shaky floor hasn't already collapsed under so much weight. If those shelves fall over, they'll probably kill someone. *Doesn't Rick realize the shelf can't hold any more books? Should I warn him?*

It's obvious Rick is completely unaware of the potential danger we're in, because the first thing he reaches for is an enormous volume of *Shakespeare's Complete Works*. If he had any idea of what was about to happen, I know he would've gone for the lighter book of sonnets instead. The air catches in my throat as I watch Rick's long fingers tenderly caress the spine of the book. *Lucky book.* He places it slowly and gently on the seventh shelf like it's the first book he's ever shelved in his life. I bite my lip. I think I'm going to faint.

Looking up, I see the corner of the shelving frame rocking perilously close to the fluorescent light fixture. I want to say something to warn Rick, but I can't seem to speak. Any second now, I know the floor is going to collapse and the metal shelving is going to topple over and crash down like a tidal wave, burying the two of us in a deadly sea of books as we clutch each other for dear life. . . .

Sounds romantic, doesn't it?

"Can I help you with something?" Rick calls from the top of the wobbly ladder.

When I wake up from my daydream, I notice that not only is the floor still perfectly intact, but that I'm staring up at Rick with my mouth drooping open and my eyes bulging like a maniac. He's probably going to call the cops any second.

So much for romance.

"Uh, no thanks," I stumble, breaking into a sweat as I look for the nearest exit. "I was just going now. . . . " I spin around in a panicked frenzy, bumping backwards into Rick's cart. A few books fall. Then a few more. One after another, the thick volumes tumble off the edge of the cart like a waterfall. I stick my arm out to stop the rest from falling to the floor, but instead I just end up pushing the cart back into Rick's ladder.

"Oh, God, I'm so sorry—" I gush, sinking to my knees, my arms flailing as I try to put the books back on the cart. *I hope they weren't in any particular order. . . .*

The ladder teeters back and forth. Rick clutches desperately onto one of the shelves to steady himself, one foot dangling in the air. "Can you move the ladder back?" he croaks, his light complexion turning a full spectrum of color. "Please?"

"Sorry . . . " I drop a pile of books and move the ladder within easy reach of the bookshelves again. Backing away from the mess, I bolt for the exit.

No big deal, I tell myself as I plow through the door, afraid to look back. *He had a one-syllable name, anyway.*

Outside, the hectic energy of Broadway helps me lick my wounds. There's nothing like instantly blending into a huge, anonymous crowd to soothe the burning pain of humiliation. I'm liking New York more every second. You can act like a goofy dork one minute and the next you can be in the middle of a crowded sidewalk where no one has the slightest idea who you are or what damage you just did. And with millions of people floating around here, the odds are statistically in your favor that there will always be someone who just did something even dumber than you did.

If my little book disaster happened in Greenwich, on the other hand, I'd never be able to leave the house again.

I stop in front of Grace Church and polish off the rest of my bagel, which has left a nice collection of poppy seeds all over the bottom of my daypack. Oh, well. The church is amazingly beautiful, like it belongs in the English countryside instead of on a busy New York street. To one side of the old Gothic church is a small medieval-looking courtyard with trees and bushes and flowers, and a grassy lawn so thick and green, it looks like a carpet. It's so peaceful. If I lived in this neighborhood I think I'd stop by here all the time.

I can't believe I'm here. . . . I'm actually on my own in New York. . . . The words run through my head like a chant as I continue on, ducking in and out of tiny vintage clothing boutiques, reading café menus, and stopping every few blocks at funky shoe stores to try on shoes so glittery and outrageous that only a rock star would buy them.

"They look *fabulous* on you," the salesgirl says at one of the stores.

"You think so?" I say, wobbling around the marble floor in a pair of six-inch red vinyl platform sneakers with black-and-white-striped soles, hoping not to break my ankles. Feeling more freakish than fabulous, I suddenly have a strong desire to join the circus.

"Absolutely," she says, pressing the tips of her violent green fingernails to her lips like she's actually serious. "They totally change your walk."

They change my walk all right—I can't move. I have to admit, though, the shoes are pretty fun to wear. My new height gives the world a different perspective. I hobble back to the bench, silently amusing myself with the fact that this girl seems to think I'm the kind of person who would buy high-heeled sneakers. *If she only knew.*

Still, I can't resist playing along. It's fun to pretend to be someone else for a little while, even if it's only to a salesgirl with sickly green nails.

"How much are they?" I ask.

The girl flashes me a gap-toothed smile. "You're in luck. They just went on sale yesterday," she says, looking at the box. "They're a real bargain at two-fifty."

"That *is* a bargain," I choke back a laugh. Two hundred and fifty dollars. That's a good chunk of the money I've saved up for my trip, and I don't even know how long it'll last me. What would I possibly use them for, anyway? Hiking?

"Will that be cash or credit?" the salesgirl asks, taking the shoes from me and taking them to the cash register.

"I don't know . . . I'm going to have to think about it," I say. "I like them and everything, but I think they might be just a little . . . I don't know . . . *too conservative* for me. I had something a little wilder in mind."

"Oh . . . ," the salesgirl murmurs, scratching the top of her shaggy head. "We have that same model in neon, if you're interested."

I wrinkle my nose. "Neon is *so* last season. Thanks for your time, though."

This is too much fun, I think to myself as I walk back outside into the steaming heat. Across the street, a purple New York University flag hangs solemnly in the humid air.

About half a block away I spot a group of people gathered in the middle of the sidewalk, huddled together as if they are looking down at something. As I get closer, a man with a pudgy face and light beard pops up, holding two fistfuls of money in the air.

"I won!" He yells loud enough so everyone on the block can hear him. "I won again!"

A guy wearing a black windbreaker and a backwards baseball cap waves two fingers in the air. "Who's in for the next round?" he asks, showing a chipped front tooth when he speaks. His eyes dart around from side to side, and he's standing behind a hastily constructed table of two milk crates and a thick, square piece of cardboard. In front of him, on the table, are three white soda caps carefully laid out in a row.

"Count me in!" shouts a woman in a jean jacket, slapping down a twenty. She bears a strangely similar resemblance to the guy in the windbreaker. "I'm gonna win some money!"

It suddenly occurs to me what's going on here. It's the shell game—a con. My dad used to warn me about con artists like these who work street corners to sucker people out of money. This is how it works: The guy behind the table has three plastic soda caps, or shells, and a little pink ball that looks like a pencil eraser. You place your bet on the table, and then he shuffles the ball around really fast from shell to shell, and when he's done mixing them up, he asks you to guess which shell the ball is under. Pretty simple, right? Apparently not. According to my dad, there are lots of Wall Street executives who lose big bucks every day on shell games. These con artists are real pros.

"Hey," the guy in the windbreaker says, nodding to me. "You want to play?"

I shake my head. There's no way I'm getting involved in this one, but I decide to stay to watch, anyway, curious to see a pro in action. He's drawn quite a crowd of people around the table, all of them shouting, excited, waving their money in the air. It seems pretty real, but if you look really close, you start to notice a few things. Like, for instance, the fact that half the people in the crowd all look related. And I'm sure the other half of the crowd are close friends. They all work together as decoys to get unsuspecting people hyped up and involved in the game. After a long day of scamming, I bet they go home and have a huge party while they divide up all their money.

Besides me, the only other people who don't seem to be part of the scam are a young, wide-eyed woman carrying a map of the city, and a guy in khaki shorts and sneakers who might be her boyfriend. Tourists.

"Any more bets?" the dealer asks.

"Right here," the tourist says, pulling two twenties out of his pocket. He has his girlfriend kiss the bills for good luck, then lays them down on the cardboard. A few of the dealer's relatives do the same. "Double or nothing," he says.

I lean over to his girlfriend. "You shouldn't bet on this," I whisper. "It's a scam."

The young woman gives me a look that's a mixture of confusion and mistrust, then primly tucks a loose strand of straight brown hair behind her ear. "Alan's won twice already," she says proudly, as if this is evidence that it's legit.

"You really should leave while you're still ahead," I insist. "Believe me, these guys are not in the business to lose."

"What guys? It's just him." The young woman turns her back on me like *I'm* the con artist and gives her guy an encouraging back rub.

"Here we go," the real con artist says, eyeing me. Pushing the sleeves of his jacket up to his elbows, he picks up the caps one at a time to show us there's nothing underneath. Then he tosses the little ball down and whips it across the cardboard from one cap to the next, so fast that it's really tough to follow. His hand jerks a few times, trying to fake us out. Alan's eyes are so wide, he's not even blinking. Finally, the ball looks like it's going to come to rest underneath the first cap, but at the very last second, the dealer does a stealth move and pops it fast under the middle one.

"Where is it?" the dealer asks, showing us his palms so I guess we won't think he's hiding the ball. All the decoys are jumping around and screaming, pointing to the first shell.

The young woman holds on to her boyfriend's elbow and whispers something in his ear. Alan squints and puckers his lips, looking back and forth indecisively, from one cap to the next. It's like he knows the ball is under the middle cap, but he's suddenly doubting himself because everyone else is pointing at the first one. He scratches his head a few times, then wrinkles his brow.

"I know where it is . . . ," I whisper to the young woman.

For the first time, she's interested in hearing what I have to say. "Where?" she asks.

Before I can answer, the guy in the windbreaker cuts me off, pointing a gold ringed finger in my face. "You know where it is?" His face is smiling, but there's an edginess in his eyes. "Show me."

I look away, not saying anything. Everyone is staring.

"Point to the right cap and you win," the shell game dealer says. "Simple as that."

"But I didn't bet," I stammer.

The dealer peels a twenty-dollar bill off the roll in his hand and puts it down in front of me. "If you're right, I'll give you this bill right here. You've got nothing to lose."

I stare at the money. Have you ever had the feeling you're being drawn into something that you know could turn out bad, but you just can't seem to help yourself? That's the sort of thing I'm going through right now. I know I should be running away from here as fast as I can, but my feet don't want to go and I can't seem to tear my eyes away from the twenty he's put in front of me. *If I pick the right cap, I can just take the money.* Can it really be as easy as he says? Maybe he lets everyone win the first round or two, to give them confidence and get them hooked on the game. That's what happened to the tourists, right?

"What's the catch?" I fold my arms in front of my chest and stare him down. *I'm streetwise, Windbreaker Guy, so don't mess with me. I know what's going on here, so don't even try to pull a fast one on me. . . .*

The dealer's eyes soften just a touch. It must be because I intimidate him. "There's no catch," he says, all smooth and friendly like a car salesman. "Are you going to guess or not?"

"Hey, that's not fair!" the young woman suddenly shouts, scowling at me. "We placed our bet like we were supposed to . . . why should she get a crack at it? She didn't even bet!"

This is getting weird. The young woman looks like she wants to deck me. This is going to get ugly. I'd better bail.

Just as I'm about to walk away, the dealer says, "I'm a fair man—so I'll tell you what I'm going to do. If the young lady shows me she has twenty dollars of her own, we'll consider that a fair bet. And if the young lady chooses the right cap, I'll give you *both* twenty dollars."

Okay, I'm officially confused. The tourists seem pretty satisfied with the deal, though, so I guess I should be, too. *I could just play this one round, take my money, and leave. It's not like I have anything to lose, right?*

"I just have to show you that I have twenty

dollars?" I ask, to make sure he didn't suddenly change the rules on me.

"Right," he answers.

"And if I pick the wrong one, I don't lose anything?"

"Right." The guy rubs his palms together impatiently. "Are you in or not, because I don't have all day."

The decoys close in around us like a flock of pigeons, and I feel all this pressure now to go through with it. "All right," I say, unzipping my day-pack. I pull a twenty-dollar bill halfway out of the pocket. "See? I have a twenty." When he seems satisfied, I shove it back in the pocket and zip it closed.

The dealer nods. "Now, where's the ball?"

I point to the middle cap.

He lifts the cap, and sure enough, the pink ball is there.

"We did it!" the young woman screams, hugging her guy and jumping up and down. "We won!"

"This is better than Atlantic City," Alan gushes. "Three times in a row!"

I couldn't care less about winning. All I want to do is get my twenty bucks and haul out of here, when I hear some woman shouting from about fifty feet away. I can't make out what she's saying, but it sounds like she's spotted a cop nearby. The decoys scatter in a thousand different directions, disappearing within seconds into the masses of people on Broadway. The dealer swipes his hand across the cardboard and picks up all the money, shoving it into his pockets. With a hard kick, the gambling table becomes nothing more than a heap of street junk—a few milk crates, a piece of cardboard, and a few soda caps. Nothing that could ever be used as evidence.

"Hey! He took our money!" the young woman shouts at her boyfriend, pounding on his chest with her fists. "Run after him!"

For a split second, it looks like Alan wants to do it, but he quickly thinks better of it. "I'll never catch the guy," he says in defeat.

Standing in the middle of the junk heap, the three of us watch numbly as the con artist runs around the corner, disappearing into the crowd without a trace.

Between nearly killing a Strand employee, losing money I never had in the first place to a con artist, and of course the big scene with my parents this morning, I think I've had just about all the excitement I can handle for one day. I head back to the apartment a little earlier than I'd originally planned, emotionally wiped out and weary from being elbowed and bumped and crowded by thousands of people rushing around. How do New Yorkers keep up with the fast pace all the time? No one ever seems to slow down, not even for a second.

I return to the cozy cocoon of Kirsten's apartment, a safe refuge from the chaotic city. Luckily, no one's there, so I can have a few quiet moments to myself. I flip through a few of Kirsten's magazines, walk around the place like it's my own, then curl up on the futon and quickly drift off to a peaceful sleep. . . .

In my dream I see a piece of cardboard stretching a mile long, covered with hundreds of white

soda caps, lined up one right after the other. Rick,
the guy at the bookstore, shuffles a pink ball from
cap to cap, practically at the speed of light. I try to
follow, but I can't. My dad towers overhead, point-
ing a disapproving finger at me. "You'd better find
it, Miranda," he says angrily. "You'd better find out
where the ball went or we're all in big trouble." In
a fever, I pick up one cap, then the next, running
up and down the sidewalk, trying to find the little
pink ball. Everyone stops and stares. "This is it—
this is the one!" I shout, lifting up the cap. To my
horror, there's nothing underneath. Someone in the
crowd hisses. "She's a loser!" a voice screams. The
crowd closes in, then everyone hurls poppy seed
bagels at my head. . . .

Suddenly, there's a loud *slam*. I'm jolted
upright, awake in a matter of seconds, my heart
pounding like a jackhammer against my rib cage.
What was that?

"Sorry," calls a voice from somewhere in the
apartment, but it doesn't belong to Kirsten. It's a
guy's voice—deep and raspy.

It must be Kirsten's roommate, Vance. I quickly
run my fingers through my tangled hair and
smooth the sleepy wrinkles out of my T-shirt. With
my head throbbing from waking up so suddenly, I
stumble out to the kitchen to see what's going on.

Sitting at the kitchen table is a tall, angular guy
in dirty jeans and a white tank top, twisting
together a few wires from the back of the cracked

stereo console. His hair is cropped short with jet-black roots and bleached-blond tips, and there's a pierced ring in his eyebrow that makes my face itch every time I look at it. Thank God he wasn't home when my parents were here. I can just imagine the look of horror on my mom's face. *Mitchell, did you see that? He has an earring in his eyebrow.*

"Dropped a speaker on the floor," the guy says, not taking his eyes off the miniature junkyard covering the kitchen table. "Didn't mean to wake you up."

"That's okay," I say, wondering how long he's been in the apartment. According to my watch, it's almost six, which means I've been sleeping for two solid hours. *Did he see me?* Dread seeps into my blood like poison. *Please tell me I wasn't sleeping with my mouth open again, drooling all over the place. How gross is that?*

"I'm Miranda," I say sheepishly, checking the corners of my mouth for moisture.

"Vance," the guy answers, shaking my hand. He turns on a small desk light and resumes his seemingly futile project of trying to piece the console back together. "How's everything going, Miranda?" he asks like I've known him for years.

"All right." I lean with my back against the edge of the door frame. "How's the stereo coming?"

Vance smacks his hands together like a mad

64

scientist and reaches for a wire cutter and a tube of Super Glue. "The CD lens is scratched, but I think I can get the tape player working. Can you believe I found this baby on the street?"

"Actually, I can," I say dryly.

Vance doesn't seem to get my joke. He looks up at me with serious brown eyes that suddenly grow wide. "Wow," he says, flashing the desk light on me. "You have the reddest hair I've ever seen."

I squint in the bright beam of light, feeling like I'm in a police lineup. "I get that a lot."

"I mean it's red-red, not orange-red."

Already, my cheeks are starting to get warm. "I take after my grandmother on my dad's side—she was Irish."

"Interesting." Vance thoughtfully scratches his stubbly chin, then clears a seat for me at the table. "Do you play bass?"

I sit down across from him. "Excuse me?"

"You know, bass guitar," he says, strumming the air with his long, bony fingers. "Do you play?"

"No."

"How about keyboards? I'm putting together a band."

"I play a little," I say. "And I can sing."

"A singing keyboard player—not bad." The little silver loop in Vance's eyebrow bobs dramatically. "We could use someone like you on backup vocals."

Someone like me. What is he talking about?

"What kind of music do you play?" I ask.

"High concept . . . we're taking modern music to a whole new level. We're making stuff that no one's ever heard before—heck, we're making stuff no one's even *thought* of." Vance leans toward me, the desk lamp highlighting the shadowy contours of his square face. "The toughest thing in the world is to be original, Miranda. You're a musician, you know exactly what I'm talking about. It seems like everything's been done before, everything's a cliché. But we broke through. We've stumbled onto something so big, we're going to be setting the musical standard well into the next millennium."

"Wow—that sounds pretty amazing," I say, not quite sure what to make of this guy who spends his free time putting shattered stereos back together with Super Glue. "So how long has the band been together?"

"About a week." Vance squirts a glob of glue and reattaches the volume knob. "We're rehearsing in a few hours for a gig tomorrow night. You should come—we need your musical expertise. We're building an empire, and you can be a founding emperor or empress, whichever you prefer."

Vance is kind of kooky, but I decide I like him. Pushing aside a few broken pieces of plastic, I lean my elbows on the table. "I'd love to be an empress in your band," I say, trying to keep a straight face.

"The only problem is, I'm going away with Kirsten, remember?"

Vance's face falls. "Oh, yeah, that's right." Picking up the cutters, he snaps a yellow wire in two. "Too bad—you could've been a part of rock-and-roll history. You missed your chance."

"At least I'll be able to tell my friends I met you." A giggle rises up from my throat, but I hold it in. "So what instrument do you play?"

"Buckets."

"Buckets?"

"Instead of drums," Vance explains. He pounds out a rhythm on the tabletop with the wire cutters. "It's just until I can afford a real set. Buckets aren't bad, though. They have a pretty good sound. You should come to our gig tomorrow night."

"I'd love to," I say.

The lock clicks, and the door opens. Kirsten plows in like a freight train, her arms weighed down by her bike helmet and two big plastic grocery bags that say I LOVE NEW YORK. The oily, comforting smell of Chinese food floods the kitchen.

"Mommy's home!" Kirsten calls cheerfully. "Are my children hungry?"

I get up to help her. "Smells great."

Vance eyes the bags of food. "Tell me you remembered the broccoli in hot garlic sauce."

"I remembered the broccoli in hot garlic sauce," Kirsten repeats like a robot.

Vance smacks his lips together. "Really?"

"No," Kirsten answers, hanging her helmet on one of the cupboard knobs. "But I got General Tso's Tofu."

"Forgiven," Vance chirps happily. "By the way, I was just telling my new friend Miranda about my gig tomorrow night."

Kirsten ties her hair into a hasty ponytail, brushing a few renegade strands of hair off the back of her damp neck. "You guys got a gig already? Where?"

"The Chiller," he answers proudly.

"I thought Sunday night was open mike night." She reaches into one of the bags and pulls out an egg roll. "I thought anyone could go up and play."

Vance shrugs. "Your point being . . .?"

"If anyone can go up and do whatever they want, then it's not really a *gig*, is it?"

"I'm feeling a lot of negative energy coming off you right now, Kirsten, and I have to say it's bringing me down." Vance pouts. "Regardless if it's open mike night or not, this gig is a prime opportunity for me to bring my music to the masses. Miranda here has shown her full support—unlike someone I know."

I smile weakly.

Kirsten rolls her blue eyes to the ceiling. "Sorry, Vance. I'll try to contain my negative energy. Can you forgive me?"

"Your sarcasm is noted," Vance says, contemplating the question seriously. "However, I'm willing to overlook it for a bite of your egg roll."

Kirsten hands him the rest of the roll and gives him a greasy kiss on the cheek. The scene is strangely domestic, like a punk version of *Leave It to Beaver.* "We're all set with the car, right?" she asks.

Vance's mouth is too stuffed to talk, but he gives us a thumbs-up sign. "Only if you two come to my gig," he finally says. "As witnesses to a new era of rock and roll."

"We'll be there," Kirsten reassures him. Grabbing the take-out bags, she heads for the living room, nodding for me to follow. "Come on, Miranda, let's give our musical genius some space to work. We've got a trip to plan."

West," I say, attacking a slippery pea pod with my chopsticks. "We should definitely head west."

Though it's still early in the evening, the apartment is already taking on the gray tones of dusk, the sun having long since dipped behind the tall apartment complex across the street. Kirsten is sprawled out on the living room floor with a beat-up road atlas of the New York metropolitan area draped across her torso.

"West. Well, that narrows it down to about thirty-five states," Kirsten says dryly. "Should we go northwest, southwest, or straight through the middle?"

"I don't care. I just want to go west." I lean my head against the side of one of the vinyl chairs and stare up at a flaky brown patch on the ceiling. "When I was a kid, every time my family went on vacation we always went either north or south. I want to see something different."

"So Virginia's out?"

Jayson. I had completely forgotten about my brother. It would be nice to see him, but how much fun can a person have with her overprotective older brother breathing down her neck? We'd be there five minutes and Mr. Finance Major would start in on me, talking about how great Yale is and trying to convince me to go back with him in the fall instead of wasting my life away on this *silly little trip.* If I'd wanted to be nagged to death, I would've stayed home with Mom and Dad.

"Virginia's out," I answer resolutely.

"Now we're making some progress." Kirsten puckers her pink lips in thought. "The other thing to consider is how far Vance's old clunker can actually take us. If it conks out on the side of the road, I'm all for abandoning it."

I brush a stray curl over my shoulder. "So he's really giving it to us? I can't believe it!"

Kirsten nods. "It's no great prize, believe me. We're doing *him* a favor by taking it off his hands." She lights a vanilla-scented pillar candle with a box of wooden matches. "Vance hardly drives the thing, and parking's really expensive around here. He keeps it in a garage in Brooklyn, where it's cheaper, but it takes a half-hour subway ride just to get to it. So I'm like, 'Vance—why do you bother? Save yourself the trouble and let us keep it—for good.' I was sort of joking, just thinking aloud, but he went for the idea."

Little tiny anxious goose bumps prickle my

skin. "Now we won't be tied to a train schedule. We can take off and go wherever we feel like going, whenever we feel like it."

"And we won't be stuck anywhere or with anyone." Kirsten gives me a languid smile. "It's pure freedom."

This is really going to happen. Two days from now, we're going to be out there, experiencing life. There's no jolt of panic as the idea penetrates my brain, but instead it seeps in gently like cool water being poured on dry soil. I have a feeling that Kirsten is the one to thank for this shift—her take-charge attitude has a way of putting me at ease. I know that when I'm with her there's nothing to worry about. She knows exactly what's going on.

Rolling lazily onto her back, Kirsten picks up a stray water chestnut from one of the containers and pops it into her mouth. "Isn't this so much better than school?"

"What—Chinese food?" I joke.

"No!" Kirsten laughs, making her sculpted cheekbones even more pronounced. "You know, being on your own. Doing what you feel like and not having to follow some rigid schedule."

"It's hard to say." I shrug. "I've only been out of school for a few weeks."

Kirsten thoughtfully licks the tips of her fingers. "I hope you don't mind me saying this, but I didn't think you'd actually do it."

"Do what?"

"You know, leave everything and take off with me," Kirsten says. "If I remember right, in school you had your whole life planned out perfectly until the age of sixty-three. You were going to go on to Yale to major in English literature and then around sophomore year you were going to meet some guy who was going to be a doctor—"

"Corporate lawyer," I correct.

"*Sorry*—corporate lawyer," Kirsten answers heavily. "And then you were going to fall madly in love and get married right out of school and have fifty babies and live happily ever after in an old farmhouse in Connecticut. Am I right?"

"Basically—but you left out a few details." I giggle. "After our honeymoon in Venice, I was going to become a celebrated professor of English literature at Yale and when I'd had a full, rewarding career, I'd become the perfect mother to our four children—two boys and two girls, alternating, two years apart. My husband would win one of the biggest trials in U.S. history and become famous and rich while always finding time to spend with his family. *And* he'd always buy me jewelry on our anniversary."

Kirsten curls her upper lip in obvious disgust. "That's twisted! Girl, you need help!"

"What's so twisted about it?" I answer, trying my best not to look offended. "Don't you ever dream about the future?"

"Well, yeah, but not in such sickening detail,"

Kirsten says. "My dreams are more along the lines of wondering if I'm going to eventually get an apartment on my own or if I should leave New York for someplace a little more laid-back or whether to have sushi or a frozen burrito for dinner. That's about as far as it gets."

"Don't you ever think about getting married?"

"No way. I'm *not* getting married." Kirsten shakes her head adamantly. "After seeing what it did to my parents, there's no way I'm making the same mistake."

I tilt my head back and close my tired eyes. I've met several people who feel the same way Kirsten does and it makes me sad. Granted, I have no idea what it's like to live through a messy divorce, but I hate to see people give up like that.

"Just because it didn't work out for them doesn't mean it can't work out for you," I argue.

"The only way I'd get married is if someone handed me a big fat contract that guaranteed nothing would ever go wrong," Kirsten says. "But there are no guarantees, so why set myself up for disaster?"

"You can't give up on marriage just because something *might* go wrong. You could be missing out on the most incredible experience of your life."

"If I don't know what I'm missing, then there's no harm done, right?"

"But what about kids?" I point out. "Don't you want kids?"

Kirsten wads up her napkin. "I've never been a fan."

I don't know what to say to this. I can't imagine not wanting kids. It's never even occurred to me that there are people who don't like kids.

My reaction must be transparent, because Kirsten suddenly waves her hands in the air and says, "Whoa—don't get all freaked out. We don't have to like all the same things, you know."

"I know," I answer, trying not to sound defensive.

"So why *did* you decide to come along, anyway?" Kirsten asks. She tosses me a fortune cookie. "Isn't this trip going to throw a wrench in your big plans for the future?"

"I don't have big plans right now," I say. "I'm taking a break."

"What about the corporate lawyer? What about the babies? They need you!"

"They're going to be waiting a long time, I think." My eyes fall on the hypnotic yellow flicker of the candle's flame. "During graduation, I was sitting there, listening to those boring speeches and looking around at everybody, when it suddenly hit me that my future was practically set in stone and that if I didn't do something soon, I wouldn't have another chance to change it."

Kirsten cracks open her cookie. "But *you're* the one who made it that way. You put the pressure on yourself. "

"Yes and no." I place my hand on the side of the candle and feel its warmth. "I mean, sure, I made up that list, but I think I wanted those things because that's what my *parents* want for me and because it's what everyone else around me seems to want. It didn't even occur to me until that moment that maybe, deep down, I had my own vision of what I want my life to be."

"So what's your vision?" Kirsten asks. "Does it still involve a corporate lawyer?"

"I don't know," I say, shrugging. "I'm trying to figure that out. It's nice to not have any definite plans, for a while, anyway."

Kirsten nods. "That's what I always say—play it by ear."

I crack open my fortune cookie. A JOURNEY OF A THOUSAND MILES BEGINS WITH ONE STEP. "These things always seem true," I say, handing my fortune to Kirsten. "What about yours?"

"Mine says, 'You like Chinese food.'"

We laugh so hard, our sides begin to ache. It's so fun being with Kirsten. I just know we're going to have a blast on the road. As different as we are, I feel like I click better with her than I ever did with any of my other friends in Greenwich— except maybe Chloe.

My eyes fall on the open atlas, its blue and red lines a complex network of veins pulsing on the page. "So where did we decide to go?" I say, finally getting control of my giggles.

"Northwest, I think."

"How far northwest?"

The corners of Kirsten's mouth curve into a smile. "I thought you didn't want to make plans."

"It's not a plan, exactly—it's more of a *direction*," I say with a sheepish grin.

Kirsten tosses her head back and laughs "Do me a favor and stop thinking ahead for once. Let's just see what happens."

The next morning is crazy. I wake up on the futon to the sound of things being banged, scraped, and dragged from one end of Kirsten's room to the other as she packs for the trip. If I didn't know better, I'd think she was building an addition for the apartment in there. The plumbing rattles ominously in between the walls. Outside, car horns are blaring, and a motorcycle engine revs with the same teeth-grinding squeal as fingernails being dragged across a blackboard.

I haven't been awake for more than five minutes and already I have a pounding headache. Hunkering down beneath my blanket, I sandwich my head between two pillows and close my eyes, wishing the world would just disappear so I can get a little more sleep.

"Aaaahhhh! What happened to my buckets?" Vance yells, his voice easily penetrating the four inches of cotton fluff I've stuck on either side of my head.

I give up.

Lifting one corner of the blanket, I take a peek at the kitchen doorway to see what's going on. From my limited point of view I can see Vance standing near the refrigerator, carrying two white buckets by the handles, wearing only a pair of dirty jeans and a dark, brooding expression. A crown of soapsuds billows over the tops of both buckets and drips onto the cracked linoleum floor.

"Why is there soap in my buckets?" he shouts.

The noise in Kirsten's room stops dead. "I needed to do a little hand-washing," she says mildly.

"Why didn't you use the sink?"

"In case you haven't noticed, the sink is full of dirty dishes," Kirsten answers.

Vance places the buckets carefully on the floor, a pained look twisting his face. "You need to treat them with respect, Kirsten. They're delicate instruments."

"No, Vance, they're buckets," she answers.

"The slightest residue can alter their sound." Vance's voice is starting to take on a higher pitch. "I have a performance tonight—what am I supposed to do?"

Kirsten lets out an aggravated sigh. "Then wash them out. Don't make such a big deal out of it, Vance."

On the street, a car alarm wails. I hum along to the musical pattern, having become very familiar with it over the course of the night. *No point in trying to get any more sleep,* I decide, throwing off the covers. *I'm up now.*

I don't hang around the apartment for long, not wanting to get in the middle of Kirsten's packing and Vance's bucket cleaning. Still groggy from a restless night of sleep, I go to the corner deli and buy another poppy seed bagel and munch on it in front of Grace Church until I'm fully awake.

On the next block I snag the last copy of the *Village Voice.* The arts section lists a bunch of art galleries in SoHo that have free viewings. I like art. I like free things. Sounds like the perfect way to spend the day.

I fall in love with SoHo the second I get there. How come my parents never brought me here before? If I had to choose anywhere in the city to live, this would be it. SoHo is smack in the middle between the East and West Villages, and close to Chinatown and Little Italy. The cobblestone streets are narrow, which slows traffic way down. Parts of the sidewalk are made of metal with holes in it, the holes filled with pretty purple and white glass so that it almost looks like Bubble Wrap. There are bronze sculptures on the street, and the buildings are low, old-fashioned warehouses with sprawling, open interiors that have hardwood floors and whitewashed walls. Famous fashion designers have boutiques in the neighborhood, among the galleries and artists' studios, the cafés and pottery shops. There's a lot to see.

I wander in and out of galleries most of the afternoon. There's one show I really enjoy that has these enormous paintings of architectural structures. I don't know much about architecture, but the vibrant red and electric-blue paint practically jump off the canvas. There is also a feminist video installation showing old commercials of fifties housewives using various cleaning products. My favorite show, though, has wax sculptures of everyday people doing everyday things. They all look so amazingly real. There are a few sculptures of tourists taking pictures, a woman doing a handstand against the wall, and even one of a guy sleeping on the floor that totally fooled me. In the corner of the gallery I see a guy in a business suit standing with his arms folded in front of his chest, staring up at the ceiling. I walk right up to him and touch his sleeve, thinking he's a sculpture, but the man suddenly moves away, looking at me like I'm a weirdo.

When I've had my fill of art, I use my subway map as a guide and walk southeast to Chinatown. The air changes almost immediately once I get close to Canal Street—it's filled with the salty, pungent smell of fish and other exotic, undefinable aromas. All the street signs bear Chinese characters along with the English translation: First Bank of China, Canal Street Jewelry Liquidators, Dr. Chang's Herbal Medicine, Noodletown Dumpling House. Striped bass swim in restaurant aquariums, right next to golden-skinned, whole-roasted Peking ducks hanging in the windows by their necks. Tiny women work food carts, selling paper cups of hot, glistening noodles for a dollar. In the open-air fish markets, men with sharp knives filet live bass right in front of you. It's enough to make me want to become a vegetarian.

The sidewalks on Canal are more crowded than any other street I've seen—even more crowded than Rockefeller Center at Christmastime. It's unbelievable. Most of the faces are Asian, but many like myself seem to be here to shop, eat, and soak up the atmosphere. New York City is wonderful. One minute you can be strolling through posh boutiques and art galleries, and the next minute you can feel like you just landed in the heart of Beijing.

I take a break from the crowds by ducking into a store called Pearl River Market. The size of the store is deceptive—from the street it looks like a simple, narrow storefront, but surprisingly the maze-like aisles run quite deep and take up many floors. Pearl River seems to have everything anyone could ever need: from TVs and stereos to cooking pots, clothes and toys, food, videos, and fun little trinkets like bamboo back scratchers and tapestry lipstick cases.

I'm not a clotheshorse by any stretch of the imagination, but the stuff they have at Pearl River makes me nuts. Pajamas, robes, and cute little shirts with mandarin collars, all in rich, silky jewel tones with hand-embroidered flower patterns and borders. The best thing, though, is the slim, full-length red silk evening dress that has this long slit up one side. It's the kind of dress that could stop traffic, even on Canal Street. Luckily most of the clothes run more narrow than standard American sizes and probably wouldn't fit too well on my medium-sized frame, which thankfully keeps me from buying out the place with the emergency credit card my dad gave me. Can you picture the look on his face when he got the bill? Not a pretty sight.

By late afternoon my feet are aching, so I opt for the subway instead of walking back. According to the map at the entrance to the Canal Street station, I'm supposed to take the 6 train uptown to Astor Place. That should bring me pretty close to Kirsten's neighborhood. I drop my token in the turnstile and wait on the platform.

Perfect timing. In seconds a silver train with a big green circle and the white number six comes barreling through the dark tunnel and pulls into the station. All the subway cars are packed nearly to capacity, but I don't feel like hanging around for the next train to come, so when the doors slide open I wedge myself inside with the other sardines.

"Next stop Spring Street," the train conductor announces over the crackly loudspeaker. "Please stand clear of the closing doors."

The doors close about three inches from my face. An anxious tingle starts at the base of my spine as I'm seized with the thought that there isn't enough air for all of us in here. I hold on to the silver railing and steady myself as the train makes a jerky start and we pull out of the station.

The car is surprisingly quiet except for a few isolated conversations here and there. Near the door that adjoins the next car is a man slumped in his seat, a baseball cap covering his face. Next to him is an elderly woman in a kerchief sitting with a bag of fresh produce on her lap. Three hyper teenage girls stand around the pole in the middle of the floor talking pretty loudly. A man with a thick mustache and gold-rimmed eyeglasses stands near me reading a newspaper, his elbow tapping my back every time he turns a page. It's interesting to see how no one on the train looks directly at anyone else. They're either reading or staring down at the floor or looking up at the advertisements above the door, but never in the middle where their eyes might meet someone else's. I stare out the black windows, ignoring the claustrophobic feeling that's making the hairs on the back of my neck stand straight up.

At Spring Street people pour out of the car like a dam breaking. I'm almost carried away in the flood. "Bleecker Street next," the conductor says. I step back inside the car just before the doors close again.

Finally . . . a little breathing room. I take in a

deep breath. Now that a few bodies have cleared, I can see the seats on the other side of the subway car. Two guys around my age sitting in the seats opposite are talking quickly in some throaty language I don't recognize. They're looking at me.

I stare down at the floor, pretending not to notice.

"Tchzata kayem—" the curly-haired one says, pointing in my direction.

Okay, so maybe those aren't his *exact* words, but that's what they sound like to me, anyway. What I wouldn't give for a translator right now, so I could find out what he's saying. Then again, maybe I wouldn't want to know.

"Yenghezna py chrellah!" the other one argues. He's a little guy with no neck whose head looks like it's resting on his shoulders. *"Veghri!"*

Out of the corner of my eye I see Curly Top shaking his head. *"Veghri? Kajfev tchzata snevngy."* He gives the little guy a push off his seat.

Little Guy shoves his hands shyly in his pockets and walks toward me. *Aren't we near Astor Place yet?* I think, tapping my toe against the floor. The train pulls into the next station, but it's still not my stop. Unfortunately, it's not their stop, either.

"Scherzat yeh zig kfohra," Curly Top commands. Then he takes out a pocket camera.

I think I know what's coming.

Little Guy snickers, inching closer to me. I keep

staring at the floor, not really knowing what else to do. Carefully, he reaches behind my back and grabs the pole I'm leaning against, so it looks like he has his arm around me, then gives Curly Top a bright smile. The camera flashes with me looking down, my face turning every shade of red.

The guys laugh, nudging each other. There's no doubt in my mind these guys plan on taking the picture back to their country so they can tell all their friends I'm Little Guy's American girlfriend.

I nearly jump out of the car when the doors finally open at Astor Place. As I leave the train, Little Guy smiles and blows me a kiss.

The contents of my backpack are strewn all over the futon, and I can't find anything remotely interesting to wear for an evening out with Kirsten's friends. Khakis, shorts, T-shirts, a flannel shirt, leggings, sweats—it's all so neutral and boring that I'm going to blend right into the woodwork like a piece of paneling.

I can see Kirsten introducing me now: *"Attention everyone—I'd like you to meet my bland friend Miranda. She's from Connecticut and has no sense of style whatsoever."* Then all her friends will give me a sympathetic hello and jot fashion tips on paper napkins and matchbook covers, slipping them to me discreetly under the table. That is, if they notice me at all.

"Help!" I whine, standing in the doorway of Kirsten's room. Almost all of her stuff is packed up into huge cardboard boxes and is ready to be put into storage. "Can I borrow something to wear?"

"Sure," Kirsten says as she puts the finishing touches on her loose French twist. She looks great

87

in her form-fitting black pants, black leather boots, and shiny blue short-sleeved shirt that zips up the front. It brings out the color of her eyes. "That box over there," she says, directing me to the far side of the room. "Take anything you want."

Blindly, I reach into the box and pull out the first thing I lay my hands on.

"I can't believe it!" I say, blinking back my surprise at the blouse I'm holding. It's one of those dreamy silk mandarin-collar shirts I saw earlier today. This one is pewter colored with black trim.

"Pearl River in Chinatown." Kirsten dabs her lips with dusty-rose lipstick.

"I know." I hold it against my body, praying it will fit. "I saw them today and went crazy."

Kirsten rummages through the box with me. "I have a skirt that goes with that. . . . Here it is." She hands me a straight black skirt that falls to just around my knees. I'm not a fan of skirts, especially short ones, but I'm totally in the mood to be different tonight. I want to seem just as stylish, confident, and exciting as Kirsten.

"Don't forget the shoes," Kirsten calls after me as I bound for the bathroom with my treasures. She hands me a sexy pair of ankle-strap sandals with high heels. "These are *great* shoes."

They're also a half-size too small, but I decide to sacrifice my feet in the name of fashion just for one night. Everything else fits pretty well, except the shirt is a little tight in the shoulders, which I can live with. Normally, I'm the first person to complain about the silly little outfits you see models wearing on the covers of magazines—impossibly short skirts, baby shirts, shoes even a stilt walker would have trouble in—all of it needing to be tugged and pulled to stay in place if you ever decide to sit down. The whole thing is so ridiculous. Still, even I have to admit, once in a while it's fun to be a slave to fashion. I just wouldn't do it every day.

We're supposed to meet Kirsten's friends at a little Indian restaurant on Sixth Street—also known as Indian Row, Kirsten tells me. Vance is practicing with his band, and we'll meet up with him later at The Chiller.

"You look fabulous," Kirsten says.

"Thanks," I say. I feel cosmopolitan, urban, maybe even a little bit sophisticated. Hopefully that's how I'll come across to Kirsten's friends.

The pedestrian light suddenly changes from WALK to a flashing DON'T WALK. I halt in my tracks, but Kirsten continues across the intersection as if she didn't notice the light change. In between the passing flurry of traffic I see her whip around, wondering where I've gone. When she spots me on the curb, I see her laughing.

"It said DON'T WALK," I say when the light changes again and I finally make it across.

"Tour-ist," Kirsten says in a singsong voice. "A flashing DON'T WALK is kind of like a yellow light—

there's still time. When it's steady, that's when you stop."

"Oh," I say with an embarrassed laugh.

On the corner of Sixth Street is a man in a ripped T-shirt holding an empty coffee cup. "Change. Spare any change?" he says to anyone who passes by. His skin is dark and leathery, weather-beaten. He looks like he needs help. I open the small evening bag Kirsten let me borrow. *There has to be some change in here. . . .*

"Don't," Kirsten whispers, pulling me away.

I freeze, a few coins clutched in my palm. "Why not?"

"He might just be a scam artist. Or a druggie."

"He looks sort of hungry," I tell her, unable to take my eyes off his sunken cheeks. "He might be for real."

Kirsten snaps the bag shut. "Trust me—most of them aren't."

"But how can you tell?" I look down at the change in my hand. How much harm could a little change do?

"He's smoking a cigarette, for one," Kirsten argues. "If he's so hungry, don't you think he'd spend his money on food and not smokes?"

Good point, I suppose. The homeless guy is onto our debate and holds out his cup to me, but Kirsten grabs me firmly by the wrist and pulls me away. I feel bad. To me, the guy looks like he could use some help, but Kirsten's lived here for a while, and she knows more about this sort of thing than I do. I guess I've got a lot to learn.

"If I do anything else dumb like that, please tell me," I say.

Kirsten puts her arm around me. "It wasn't dumb. I think it's kind of refreshing, actually. You're doing fine. My friends are going to love you."

Sixth Street between First and Second Avenues is a spectacular sight with its row of Indian restaurants lined up one right next to the other. Window after window there are men with turbans inside sitting on pillows playing strange-looking stringed instruments and drums. Teenagers dressed in suits stand outside, offering coupons and free appetizers if you eat at their family's restaurant. Painted posterboards display competing specials at unbelievably low prices. It's impossible to decide where to go.

"Urban legend has it that all the restaurants share one big kitchen," Kirsten tells me.

"I wouldn't be surprised—they all have the same name," I joke. Already we've passed a Taj, a Taj Palace, a Taj II, and a Taj Mahal.

"Have you ever had Indian food?" she asks.

"Not really," I say. "My mom made a vegetable curry once, but I don't think that counts."

A blissed-out look washes over Kirsten's face. "Oh, it's *so* good! You are going to love it." We step up to the front door of one of the Taj restaurants, where a teenager seems extremely pleased by our choice. "This is my favorite place," Kirsten says. "They give you all kinds of free stuff."

A well-dressed man with a reserved smile greets us inside the tiny restaurant. "Welcome," he says, bowing slightly.

While Kirsten explains that we're meeting people here, I take in the elaborate decor. Every square inch of the walls and ceiling are plastered with shiny, glittery, hanging decorations made of gold, blue, and red tin foil and dozens of strings of colored Christmas lights. The effect is sort of like a magical, sparkling tunnel. The man leads us to the back of the restaurant, where four tables covered in pink tablecloths are placed end to end. Most of Kirsten's friends are already there waiting for us. I stay behind her a little, the same way my sister Abigail hid behind my dad in Kirsten's kitchen.

"Hey, guys!" Kirsten calls happily. She goes around the table, kissing everyone on the cheek, just like they do in Europe. "Everybody, this is Miranda."

I'd planned on smiling brightly and saying something witty, but the size of the group just sucks the confidence right out of me. A weak smile and a mumble is the best I can do right now. Everyone seems friendly, though, and they give me a warm welcome. As the honorary guest, Kirsten gets to sit at the head of the table, while I get stuck at the opposite end, next to an empty seat.

"I like your shirt, Miranda," says the blond woman sitting to my right. She has delicate bones and the slightest trace of a southern accent in her voice. I wish I could remember her name.

"Thanks," I answer with an awkward smile. "I borrowed it from Kirsten. The whole outfit, actually—even the shoes."

That was a dumb thing to say . . . why couldn't you just say 'thanks'?

"Kirsten has great clothes," she answers politely.

Small talk is the worst. My mouth suddenly feels like it's stuffed with wads of cotton. I take a sip from my water glass. Kirsten already has most of the people at the other end of the table completely engrossed in a story she's telling about having to deliver a live chicken to an apartment on the Upper East Side. I study the decorations on the wall, feeling myself dissolve into the sparkling camouflage.

Kirsten delivers the punchline with perfect comic timing, and everyone laughs. It's intriguing the way she's so comfortable in her own skin. Kirsten's the kind of person who can make herself at home anywhere, the kind of person who makes every place her own. I'd give anything to be that way.

"I'm sorry, I didn't catch your name," the woman to the right of me says.

94

"Miranda," I say in between gulps of water. I force my cold lips to curve into a smile. "I'm sorry, I didn't catch yours, either."

"Darcie," she says. She motions toward the sleek Asian woman sitting next to her. "This is Tomiko."

Tomiko's black chin-length hair has shocking streaks of white that spread out from the top of her head like a starfish. "It's nice to meet you, Miranda," she says warmly. "So you and Kirsten are taking off tomorrow. Is this your first time traveling cross-country?"

"Yeah. I'm really excited," I say.

"I did it a few years ago with my older sister," Tomiko answers. "We almost killed each other, but we still had fun."

"I've always wanted to drive across the country," Darcie says, elegantly draping a pink cloth napkin across her lap, "but only if I could stay in nice hotels. I'm not interested in sleeping in a tent or in the back seat of a car. Where are you and Kirsten going to stay?"

"We don't know yet. We're just going to wing it."

Tomiko laughs. "That sounds like Kirsten. If you want to sleep with a roof over your head every night, then you'll have to make the plans, because I guarantee you Kirsten won't think of it. She could plop down in the middle of a swamp if she had to and be asleep in three minutes."

Listening to the various conversations around the table, I start to piece together, bit by bit, everyone's story. I find out that Darcie is an actress/dancer from Austin, Texas, who just auditioned for a Broadway show; Tomiko's parents have refused to pay her college tuition if she continues to study poetry; the academic-looking guy sitting next to Kirsten is Nathan, an architecture student at Cooper Union, who recently developed an allergy to shellfish; Jolene, his dreadlocked girlfriend, hates her part-time job at a coffee bar and can't wait until she can finally paint full-time; and then there's Dean, who doesn't seem to have any prospects whatsoever, but enough charm to finesse his way through any situation. He reminds me of some of the kids I went to school with.

"Should I keep waiting or should I order?" Kirsten asks.

"Order," Dean says. "He'll be along soon."

Kirsten orders for us, using words that give me no indication whatsoever as to what we will be eating. It seems like only moments later when two waiters return, carrying silver trays. "Complimentary appetizers," one of them says in a musical voice as he places a plate in front of each of us.

"What is all this?" I whisper to Darcie, pointing to the various fried tidbits staring up at me. I'm not a picky eater, but it's a little intimidating.

Darcie kindly helps me out. "That one is fried banana, and the one next to it is a *pakora*, which is like a vegetable fritter, and that turnover thing is a *samosa*. It's filled with potatoes and peas. It's my favorite." She reaches across the table for the condiment carousel. "These sauces are pretty good with it. Watch out for the green one. It's hot."

She wasn't kidding. I put a little of the green sauce on the *pakora* and I thought my head was going to explode. There was a sweet brown sauce, too, which I liked. The best, though, was the *samosa*, with its crisp, golden crust and soft, spicy insides. I could eat about a hundred of those.

In the middle of the appetizers, Kirsten suddenly stands up. "There he is!" she shouts. "It's nice of you to finally show up!"

"Sorry—work ran a little late."

I look up from my fried banana to see Kirsten dragging her friend toward me. He's wearing an army-green T-shirt and a beaded choker that looks embarrassingly familiar.

"Miranda," Kirsten says with a smile. "Meet my dear friend Rick."

I guess even the Big Apple can be too small sometimes.

"Rick works at a bookstore," Kirsten says proudly. "The Strand."

I know. Boy, do I know.

I collect whatever scraps of dignity I have left and shake Rick's hand, pretending I've never seen him before in my life. "It's a pleasure to meet you, Rick."

Kirsten gives my shoulder a firm squeeze. "Miranda is a bookstore nut," she says, seating him in the empty chair right next to me. "I'm sure you guys will have lots to chat about."

Gee, thanks, Kirsten.

While the waiter brings out appetizers for Rick, I quickly calculate the odds that Rick recognizes me from yesterday's tragic bookshelf mishap. It was during the day. I was wearing jeans. He was on a ladder. Millions and millions of people must go to The Strand every day. Maybe he *did* get a good look at me, but this restaurant has low lighting, I'm dressed up, and I look a whole lot different straight on than I do from an aerial view. I'm guessing, anyway.

The chances of Rick recognizing me are pretty slim.

Then again, I really made a huge mess. People tend to remember things like that. And Kirsten told him I liked books. Dead giveaway.

So what. A lot of people like books. It doesn't mean anything. . . . God, I didn't even stick around to see if he was all right. . . . What kind of person am I?

If Rick *does* recognize me, he certainly isn't letting on. He smiles pleasantly at me and digs into his appetizers. I watch the choker move up and down his neck while he eats.

"How was work today?" Darcie asks him.

"Busy," Rick says. "We got this big shipment in yesterday, and my boss wanted them all shelved by Monday. It was a total nightmare."

And I would've been done a lot sooner if some ditzy redhead hadn't tried to kill me. . . . I'm waiting for Rick to go into the grisly details of our unfortunate meeting, but he ends up changing the subject to Darcie's Broadway audition instead. It's her second callback for an original musical production called *Please Don't Sing to the Animals*, about two young lovers who get locked in the Bronx Zoo overnight.

"The casting director said I had a good shot at

playing a hippopotamus in the chorus," Darcie says. "I'm not sure I should take that as a compliment."

"Everyone needs to start somewhere," Rick says.

"Yeah," I add, putting in my two cents. Rick and Darcie look up at me, clearly startled that I've spoken. My brain goes into overdrive searching for something meaningful to add to my brilliant commentary. "Yeah . . . that's so true. . . "

Nice going, Einstein.

The rest of our food arrives, and not a moment too soon. Dish after dish makes its way around the table: tandoori chicken, rice, curried vegetables, lamb in a cream sauce, chickpeas and potatoes, spinach with homemade cheese cubes, sautéed cauliflower, and this incredible flatbread called *naan*, piping hot from the oven and brushed with melted butter. Everything tastes delicious, even the foods I normally hate like cauliflower and lamb. The spices are complex and interesting and so hot at times that I'm sure my body temperature's shot up a few degrees. Or maybe it's because I keep picturing Rick in my mind's eye holding on to that metal shelf for dear life.

The atmosphere at the table is relaxed and mellow as everyone dives in. I want to say something to Rick, but after that last comment, I don't want to open my mouth for fear of what will come out. He seems very much inside himself, like I can be sometimes. Maybe he feels as awkward as I do. From the other side of the table Kirsten notices that sparks aren't exactly flying between us. She scrunches her face at me and nods in his direction as if to say, *Talk to him! Say something!*

All right! I scrunch back. *I'll try . . .*

"So . . . Rick . . ." Beads of sweat slither down my back. "Do you like to read?"

Rick rips a piece of *naan* in two. "Yeah. I used to read a lot before I took this job at the bookstore. . . . Now when I go home, the last thing I feel like looking at is a book."

Kirsten is still eyeing me, so I press on. "I know what you mean," I say, compulsively plucking stray crumbs off the tablecloth. "I spent a lot of summers working at a pizza joint. To this day, the smell of oregano makes me break out in hives."

While Rick politely laughs at my lame joke, I can't help watching the beaded choker nestle into the hollow of his throat. "An allergy to pizza," he says. "That's tragic."

"A book allergy is even worse," I answer, regaining a bit of confidence. "It sounds like you're well on your way to one if you're not careful."

"I'm going to take care of that pretty soon." Rick scoops up a bit of rice with his bread. "Every summer I like to tackle a really huge book. It gives me a sense of accomplishment."

A guy with goals . . . I like that. "So what are you reading this summer?"

"I haven't decided yet," he says. "Do you have any suggestions?"

My mouth suddenly goes dry. I practically live and breathe books—so why am I drawing a total blank?

"How about *The Complete Works of William Shakespeare*?" I blurt, remembering the thick volume Rick placed on the top shelf before I nearly killed him. The second the words leave my throat I'm already cringing inside. If Rick didn't remember me before, he certainly will now.

Rick narrows his eyes, as if he's trying to remember me from somewhere. "I read the plays last summer," he says distractedly. "But I never got to the sonnets."

Ambitious and brainy, too . . . not to mention terminally cute, I tell myself, hoping the dim lighting is still working to my advantage. *Let's just hope he has a horrible memory. . . .*

By the time the waiters come to clear our plates, the eight of us have managed to stuff ourselves to the gills—except Darcie, who for some odd reason doesn't want to gain weight in case she gets the hippo job. Figure that one out. Even with all we ate, there's still a ton of food left. As a waiter takes away my plate, I tell him to wrap up all the leftovers on the table. With the rhythm of our conversation broken, an uncomfortable silence falls between us. Rick stares down at the table, I look up at the lights.

"So," Rick says, breaking the long silence. "Are you going to The Chiller with the rest of the gang?"

I nod. "Are you going?"

Rick smiles shyly. "I am now."

After dinner we all decide to walk the ten or so blocks to The Chiller. I lag behind the group, weighed down by the big plastic bag of leftovers the waiter gave me, hoping to see the man with the change cup on the corner, but he's not there. A few blocks further down we pass a woman sleeping in a cardboard box, a grocery cart filled with empty cans and scraps of clothes parked near her head. I quietly set the bag of leftovers beside her and walk on, hoping she'll wake up before the food gets too cold.

"Where'd you disappear to?" Kirsten says when I rejoin her at the stoplight. "I thought we were going to have to send out a search party."

"There's so much to look at, I get a little distracted sometimes," I fib. I get the feeling she might not approve of what I've just done, so there's no reason to bring it up.

"Well, keep up! I can't lose you now—you're my copilot!" Kirsten loops her arm through mine. "Are you having a good time?"

"The best," I answer happily. "I can't imagine any place I'd rather be."

At home right now, the house is settling down into its predictably depressing Sunday night murmur, with Mom in her pajamas already and Dad finishing up the Sunday crossword, falling asleep with his pen still in his hand. Abigail is probably gabbing on the phone, and if I were there, I'd be in my room warding off the blues by writing in my journal, reading a good book, or stretching out on the couch watching TV shows about young, hip urbanites having the time of their lives. But instead of sitting at home, watching all the action, I'm out here actually *experiencing* it. No curfews, no restrictions, no rules. I've waited for this my whole life.

Too bad we're leaving tomorrow. I really like it here.

Kirsten leans over and whispers in my ear, "So, did you hit it off with Rick? He's nice, isn't he?"

I nod discreetly on both counts. I'm dying to confess to Kirsten about the disaster in The Strand and the unbelievable coincidence that Rick turned out to be her friend, but there are too many people around, and I keep catching a glimpse of Rick's army-green T-shirt out of the corner of my eye. Even though I'm practically bursting inside, I guess the confession will have to wait.

"Is this the one?" Dean points to the plain black door of an old warehouse building with no signs or windows. "I always forget where it is."

"You have to look for the Dumpster," Jolene answers. Sure enough, right against the brick wall is a big green trash bin with THE CHILLER written in squiggly black spray paint.

My heart sinks. This hardly looks like the cool club I had envisioned.

We make our way down a steep set of dark stairs leading into the basement of the building, with me clutching Kirsten's arm so I don't kill myself in these heels. *Okay, this is definitely going to be an experience,* I think somewhat hesitantly, my ankles teetering with each step.

A thin, watery beam of blue light comes into view at the bottom of the stairs. It doesn't take long to figure out where The Chiller gets its name. The entrance to the club is a stainless-steel door that's several inches thick with a lever for a door handle, the kind you'd see in a meat locker. And that's exactly what it used to be—a big old freezer for meat. You'd think a place like this would be sort of grungy and smelly, but all the doors and walls are gleaming and shiny, even in the dim blue light.

In one room there's a coffee and juice bar. It turns out that this is where Jolene works when she's not painting, so she gets us in for free. The room just beyond the bar is a performance space with a stage that looks like it was once a freezer compartment. Little round tables are scattered all over the dark room, each lit with votive candles. In the back of the club, near the bathrooms, is a camera projecting onto the wall whatever is happening onstage. Right now, there's just a technician setting up a few microphones and speakers.

The place is filling up quickly, so we snag two of the tables near the stage and push them together. Darcie, who disappeared when we first came in, suddenly reemerges from the back room.

"They have glow-in-the-dark lights in the bathroom," she reports with a mischievous giggle. "I can't tell you what a scary experience *that* was."

Kirsten takes the chair on my left and Dean reaches for the one on my right, when Rick suddenly appears, sliding into the seat. "If this place used to be a freezer you'd think they'd be able to at least get a little air-conditioning in here . . . ," Rick says, pretending not to notice Dean's sour grin.

"It *is* pretty hot in here," I answer with a straight face, acting as if I didn't catch Rick's sly maneuver. A drop of perspiration trickles down the back of my neck and it's not just because of the humidity. Is it my imagination, or is this guy interested?

"There he is," Kirsten says, waving at the stage. "Vance! Over here!"

Vance spots us and struts over to our table, a pair of drumsticks sticking out of the back pocket of his jeans. "I waited by the door for a while. I thought you were going to bag on me."

"And miss rock-and-roll history?" Kirsten says, incredulously. "Are you nuts?"

Smiling, Vance reaches into his pocket and pulls out several slips of paper and a pen. "If you want to sign up you'd better hurry—they're almost about to start."

Tomiko, Darcie, and Kirsten each grab a slip. "Do you want to go up, Miranda?" Kirsten asks, writing her name on the slip of paper.

"Go up where?" I ask.

"On the stage."

I wince. "And do what?"

"Sing, dance, tell stupid jokes—whatever," she says. "It's open mike."

"No thanks," I say, shaking my head adamantly. Oral reports in school were enough to make me break out in a rash, never mind the pressure of performing spontaneously in front of a room full of sophisticated New Yorkers. "I'll just stay here and watch."

"Come on," Kirsten presses. "Be adventurous."

Vance gives my shoulder a light nudge. "Come on, Miranda. You're a musician. You need to express yourself or your art will die inside of you, and that, I think, would be tragic."

I give the room the once-over. It's packed. "No way."

"Whatever." Kirsten shrugs. I can tell she's disappointed in me. "It's your call."

Vance takes the slips of paper and slinks away,

leaving me aching with regret while Kirsten turns and talks to Darcie like I'm not even here. *So what if I don't want to go onstage,* I argue with myself, reaching for the candle and swirling the melted wax around the insides of the glass container until it hardens to a thick edge. *What's the big deal?*

A man appears onstage dressed in a long, red-sequined gown, false eyelashes, and a three-foot-high platinum-blond beehive wig. "Welcome to open mike night at The Chiller, everybody! I'm your host, Miss Scarlett!" After a few really bad *Gone With the Wind* jokes that leave the audience groaning, Miss Scarlett reaches into a top hat and pulls out a slip of paper. "Our first performer this evening is . . . Mr. Doug!"

The crowd sits in hushed silence as the fleshy-faced Mr. Doug ambles into the spotlight. He adjusts the microphone and clears his throat twice, then, opening his mouth and thumping on the top of his head with his knuckles, Mr. Doug proceeds to play the theme from *The Lone Ranger*, the empty echoes of his head sounding each crisp note. Everyone in the room goes ballistic. For his grand finale, Mr. Doug does a jazzy rendition of "Stars and Stripes Forever."

Miss Scarlett calls Tomiko's name next. She recites some of her own poetry, which is really good. They seem more like stories than poems, vivid images sort of washing over you like warm sunlight. It's great the way she can just go up there and share her deepest thoughts with total strangers, not being afraid at all of what others might think.

"Great job," I tell her when she returns to our table. "You're so brave. I could never go up there."

Jolene brings a free round of carrot and celery juice to everyone at our table. It tastes pretty awful to me, but Tomiko takes a hearty drink. "I love reciting for an audience," she says. "I can't imagine spending hours and hours on my work only to have it sit in a drawer unread by anyone but me. Poems are meant to be shared."

Another poet goes up onstage, then a juggler who isn't very good, followed by a kooky playwright who reads the rough draft of his first play, acting out not only the role of the alien who's made a crash-landing on Earth, but also the part of the circus clown who tries to help tow the alien back to his home planet of Mercury.

Rick catches me zoning out during the alien play and leans over. He smells of old books and soap. "Not interested in space travel?"

"Not when it involves clowns," I say with a shy smile. Holding the glass votive with both hands, I stare down at the flame. "They give me the creeps."

"Me, too," Rick admits, the flickering shadows outlining the smooth contours of his jaw. He

111

opens his mouth to say something, but he hesitates, then falls silent.

Under the table, I feel the slightest brush of Rick's jeans against my leg as he shifts in his seat, the brief electric touch leaving my heart thundering in my chest. In the hazy glow his lips look so soft, so . . . kissable. *This can't be my imagination . . . something's going on here, isn't it? Or maybe I'm just reading into things . . . again.* I mean, it's not like I had guys crawling all over me in high school—in fact, it was just the opposite. Chloe, who definitely had her share of boyfriends, said that smart, beautiful girls intimidated guys, and I scared them off. To be honest, I think she was just trying to spare my feelings.

"I can't believe how hot it is in here," Rick finally says, wiping his hand across his brow. Eyes glued to the stage, he seems almost afraid to look at me. "Do you feel like stepping out for a little fresh air?"

Okay, now that *was a definite move. . . .*

You'd think I'd spring out of my chair and make a mad dash for the door, but instead I sort of hang back, not saying anything while my stomach does somersaults. The stuffy air is making my head feel like a bowling ball. This whole thing is freaking me out. . . . I mean, what's going to happen out there? Are we going to talk? Is he going to kiss me? I can hardly imagine anything more romantic than to be kissed on a beautiful summer

112

night in New York City . . . but why would Rick want to kiss me? I mean, he's *gorgeous.* Maybe he has recognized me after all and now has a secret plan to get me out on the second-floor ledge, hanging by my fingertips, so I'll know what it feels like to be left stranded, dangling in midair. . . .

Oh, shut up already shouts a voice inside my head. *Be adventurous for once in your life.*

"Fresh air would be nice," I say, bounding to my feet. Rick smiles and leads me through the maze of tables, past the bar, and out the heavy steel doors. We climb the dark, creaky stairs in silence, me gripping the railing with both hands, stepping gingerly in the too-small heels I'm beginning to loathe.

Outside, the sky is teetering on the edge between dusk and night, barely holding on to a perfect shade of jeweled blue. The impending darkness softens the hard edges of the concrete buildings around us, the lights from each apartment glittering overhead like stars. And just when I think a summer evening in New York couldn't be more perfect, a burst of balmy evening air drifts off the Hudson River, bringing along with it the pungent smell of rotting garbage from the nearby Dumpster. Yuck.

"So much for fresh air," I joke, leaning back against the wall.

Rick laughs, shoving his hands in his pockets, kicking at the ground with his black leather boots.

He cocks his head to the side, letting a blond strand fall across his eyes. "Can I ask you a question?"

"Yeah . . . " I lace my fingers behind my back. "Sure."

"Ever since dinner, I've had this nagging feeling I've seen you somewhere before, but I couldn't quite remember where . . . then, when we got to the club, it hit me."

Oh boy . . . here we go . . .

"Were you by any chance at The Strand yesterday?" he asks.

Busted.

Repeatedly pressing my back into the bricks, I hope to discover some long-forgotten secret trapdoor that will help me to exit gracefully from this awkward situation. Better yet, maybe I should just bang my head against the wall until I'm knocked unconscious. It's tough to be embarrassed if you're passed out cold.

"Uh . . . " I stare into his eyes, trying to read what's going on behind them. One minute I think he's just making friendly conversation, and the next minute it looks like he's wondering where he can find a tall scary ladder to put me on.

"Yeah, that was me," I answer, laughing and shrugging coyly. "Oooops, I guess you found me out."

Please don't hurt me . . . please don't hurt me . . . please don't hurt me . . .

"I knew it!" Rick says, nodding. "Why didn't you say anything?"

My cheeks blush hotly. "Would you?"

"I guess not," Rick smirks, drawing closer. Moving over to a spot on the wall right next to me, he leans against a swirling patch of graffiti. "I wanted to talk to you, but you ran away too fast."

I swallow hard, but try to look casual. "Oh, yeah?"

"Yeah," he says, softly. "I wanted to give you the bill for all those books you wrecked."

My stomach drops, and my face falls.

"I'm just kidding." Rick's eyes spark with laughter. "Sorry, I couldn't help myself."

"Really funny," I answer dryly. "I suppose I deserve that."

Rick shakes his head and touches me lightly on the shoulder. "No, you don't. You didn't wreck anything—I'm sorry." His face grows serious. "I was sorry you ran off. I didn't think I'd ever see you again. And then today, I go to Kirsten's party and you're here. Weird."

"You say that like it's a bad thing."

"No, it's good," Rick whispers, licking his lips. "It's definitely good."

Somewhere along the line I've forgotten to breathe. Rick leans slightly forward, staring deeply into my eyes as he tilts his gorgeous face down toward me. Blood quickens in my veins, and I close my eyes, feeling his warm breath as he inches closer.

115

Several feet away, a metal door creaks open.

"There you are!" I hear Kirsten say. "I've been looking everywhere for you two."

Startled, I open my eyes. Rick's back straightens. He gives Kirsten a weary smile. "We needed a little air," he explains, his face reddening.

Within seconds Kirsten has managed to wedge herself between us, casting a suspicious eye from me to Rick and back again. "Vance is almost up. He'll be upset if you miss him," she says, grabbing me by the wrist. Before I have a chance to say anything, she yanks me toward the door. I look over my shoulder at Rick, who's just standing there, shaking his head.

"What'd you do that for?" I demand, my lips swollen and burning, wishing they were still outside with Rick and the beautiful New York City sky. Being someone who's only been kissed about three times in her life, moments like this don't come along too often.

"Believe me, I did you a favor," Kirsten whispers, leading me down the stairs. "You've got to watch out with Rick. I love him to pieces, but he can be a real dirty dog sometimes. I should've warned you earlier, but I didn't think he'd have the nerve to try anything with me around."

I groan inwardly, unsure whether to thank Kirsten or yell at her. "He *seems* nice," I argue sullenly. The guy likes books—how bad can he be? "He didn't do anything *wrong*. . . ."

"He didn't get a chance to," Kirsten says, leading me back inside the club. "Let's just say he didn't earn the nickname *The Octopus* because of his scuba-diving experience. Don't be mad."

"I'm not mad," I mutter. "Just disappointed."

"Please, Miranda, don't get worked up over someone like Rick," Kirsten says, meeting my eyes. "As soon as you get out in the real world guys are going to be tripping all over themselves to get to you. You're going to be fighting them off with a stick."

I roll my eyes at her. "Somehow I doubt that."

Go, Vance!" Kirsten and I scream at the stage.

Vance gives us a small, serious wave, absorbed in the task of placing his buckets in a perfect acoustical configuration. The tall, pale guitarist hunches awkwardly over her guitar, her shaking fingers silently practicing the chords. Dressed in an oversized psychedelic caftan, the lead singer stares at the back of the room, appearing to go into a trance.

"Are they any good?" I ask Kirsten, who picks up Vance's rebuilt, Frankenstein stereo off the floor and puts it on the table. Glue-filled cracks run through every part of the case like veins in marble, holding all the bits and pieces together.

"Good? No, not at all," Kirsten answers with her usual frankness. She pops in a fresh tape and presses the record buttons, which are being held in place with a piece of Scotch tape. The tape reels warble a little, then slowly chug their way into motion. "I'm going to miss that brat." Kirsten sighs. "Did you hear me, Vance?" she says, speaking into the stereo's recording microphone. "I'm going to miss you."

Just for the record, Kirsten was totally right about Rick trying to scam me. A few minutes before Vance's band went up, Rick came slinking back in, but this time instead of taking a seat near me he sidled up next to Darcie. Out of the corner of my eye I watched him cozy up to her, whispering in her ear. The next thing I know Rick's leading Darcie by the hand toward the stairs. I can't tell you how lucky I feel that Kirsten saved me from this loser. I really don't know what I was thinking. What would I do without her?

Onstage, Vance slips on a pair of dark sunglasses and instantly transforms into a rock star. "Thank you for coming out tonight. Here's a little tune we've been working on. I think some of you might be familiar with the words."

Counting off, Vance pounds out a rhythm on the buckets. *Thud, thud, thud, whack-whack, thud, whack* . . . The sound of plastic being beaten mercilessly hardly travels further than the edge of the stage, but Vance grooves on with intense concentration, his tongue sticking out of one side of his mouth. The guitarist joins in, almost absentmindedly, and the chords she hits sound more like accidental noise than music. When the singer recovers from her trance she opens her eyes and belts out with a mournful wail, "Mary had a little lamb . . .

119

yes, she did . . . and that little lamb's fleece was as white, I said it was as white as *snow* . . . "

Kirsten and I exchange pained looks. It's pretty awful. Vance was right—no one's done this sort of thing before, and there's obviously a good reason why.

"A-lamb, a-bam, a-ram . . . little lamb lamb . . . Scary Mary quite ordinary, how does your little lamb know . . . "

The guitarist drops her pick and suddenly stops playing altogether, scouring the floor to see where it landed. Turning around to see what's going on, the singer loses her train of thought, and Vance tries to hold on to the beat while the whole band disintegrates around him.

When the song comes to a mind-numbing end nearly ten minutes later, Kirsten jumps to her feet, applauding wildly. "Bravo! That was brilliant!" she shouts, as if it was all intentional. I stand up, too, along with everyone at our table, cheering Vance on. The rest of the room joins in.

"Thank you, New York—good night!" Vance shouts into the mike. His face is glowing.

"Wasn't that just lovely?" Miss Scarlett says, returning to the stage with the top hat full of names. "I wouldn't want to follow *that* one." Reaching a silk gloved hand into the hat, Miss Scarlett pulls out another slip of paper. "Our next performers are . . . Kirsten Greene and Miranda Burke!"

Before my brain has a chance to soak up

what's really going on, Kirsten's yanking me toward the stage. "I told you I didn't want to go up there," I protest.

Kirsten laughs, squinting in the spotlight. "Come on," she mutters through pressed lips. "Think of this as a bonding experience."

"Please don't make me do this. . . . "

Seeing the look of terror in my eyes, Kirsten enlists the help of Tomiko and Jolene. For a split second my fear subsides, and I go to sit back down, when Kirsten grabs my wrist and resumes dragging me to the stage. Clearly, she's not letting me off the hook.

How can she be so calm? I wonder as I climb the stairs behind her and the rest of the girls, my nerves all jangly and weird. Pure, stinging fright rages in the base of my spine, radiating throughout the rest of my body.

"What are we going to do?" I whisper.

"You'll see," she says, arching one black eyebrow mysteriously.

People are shouting and applauding, but in my ears it sounds as if they are clapping in a tin can. The atmosphere suddenly turns foggy and white. My breath is raspy and shallow.

Kirsten takes the mike. I stand directly behind her so only the people on the extreme left and right of the stage can see me. Tomiko stands to my left. Jolene hands a cassette tape to the technician, then scurries across the stage to my right.

"Thanks everybody," Kirsten says, bowing her head. She's such a natural onstage—she looks like she's spent her whole life in the spotlight. "Hi, I'm Kirsten, and these are my backup singers, The Kirstenettes, and we'd like to do a little song for you." Jolene signals to the technician, who hits the tape right on cue. A drumbeat fills the room. Kirsten pulls her head and shoulders back and assumes the kind of confident stance you only see in born performers. Drawing her arms out straight on either side, Kirsten starts snapping her fingers in time to the beat. "It goes a little something like this. . . . "

Through the sound system, Tina Turner's voice is carried out over the crowd, singing an old song from the sixties I may have heard once on the oldies radio station my dad listens to. I don't know the words at all, but Kirsten obviously does, choosing not to lip-synch to Tina but to plow right over her with her own voice. The effect is something like a freight train coming at you from both sides.

Jolene and Tomiko slip into the roles of Kirstenettes so perfectly, they must've done it before. They sway and snap and spin with perfect choreography, singing the backup parts in all the right places. I stand there like a dolt behind Kirsten, while Jolene and Tomiko bump into me.

They're so cool, and I look like a total idiot.

"Do this," Jolene whispers, pausing so I can

jump in. She takes two steps to the right, two to the left, one to the right, one to the left . . . repeating the sequence with arms swinging in the same direction. It takes me a few rounds to get it right, but I finally break into the rhythm, my motions feeling stiff and robotic against Jolene's smooth moves.

Kirsten wails into the microphone, strutting across the stage with the mike stand raised above her head, shaking and shimmying for the benefit of the guys in the front row. Her presence is so captivating, I almost lose count of the beat, but quickly regain my sense of timing. Me and Tomiko and Jolene are actually starting to flow like one unit. *Hey, this isn't so bad . . . actually, it's pretty fun.*

I'm almost sad when the music ends. "Thank you!" Kirsten shouts, taking a deep theatrical bow. The crowd jumps to their feet, clapping wildly, sharp whistles and shouts cutting through the air. Even Miss Scarlett gives us a curtsy.

Kirsten steps back to join her Kirstenettes. "You're a good sport, Miranda," Kirsten says breathlessly as we take a bow, arms linked together. "I *knew* you had guts."

I can't stop smiling long enough to answer.

Just a few more things to pack and I'll be ready to go," Kirsten says the next morning, fluttering around the kitchen all cheery and nice. She's been up for hours and already bought me a poppy seed bagel for breakfast. I don't know how she can be so awake this early in the morning.

"Uh-huh," I mumble, munching on the bagel. While she packs and cleans, I bury myself in a celebrity gossip magazine I found under the coffee table. Even though the magazine is over a year old, it's still fun to look at because you know how everything will turn out. The movie hyped on page four will end up bombing. The famous Hollywood couple who got married after dating for only a week will end up getting divorced four months later. It's almost like being able to see into the future.

The louver doors on the left side of the kitchen slide open, and Vance tumbles out in a pair of gray sweatpants, sleepily rubbing his eyes. He rinses out a mug from the sink and pours himself a cup of black coffee.

Kirsten gives him a curious, sidelong glance. "You're still here? I thought you were in Brooklyn getting the car for us."

Vance takes a leisurely sip and scratches his bare chest. "Something amazing happened last night after you guys left. This woman came up to me and said she really liked the band's sound. It turns out that she's been working this past week as a temp at Polygram Records. She said she could pass on a demo tape for us."

A shadow darkens Kirsten's eyes. "And?"

"Well, if she gets it to the right people and they like it, we could have a recording contract."

"That's not what I meant." Kirsten brushes a stray hair off her forehead. There's an ominous edge to her voice. "What exactly does this have to do with you getting the car?"

They stare at each other for a minute, tension silently building between them. I pretend to be minding my own business, but obviously something's going on.

Vance lowers his tousled head and gives Kirsten a sheepish look. "We need equipment, Kirsten. . . . I could use a set of real drums."

Kirsten clenches her fists so tightly, they're shaking. "You said we could have the car!" she shouts. "You're going to ditch us for that stupid band?"

Judging from the way Vance flinches, it looks as though Kirsten's insult has hit its target. "It's nothing personal—selling the car is just the quickest way for me to get some money. You can buy it if you want."

An exasperated growl explodes from Kirsten. "Like I have the money! If I had the money I wouldn't have thought of using your car in the first place!"

"I'm really sorry," Vance says, shaking his head. "I don't want you mad at me—if it means that much to you, just take it. I don't care."

The anger seems to slowly hiss out of Kirsten like a leaky balloon. "Never mind. I'll think of something." In a daze, she retreats back to her room and slams the door shut.

I pretend to be engrossed in the magazine, not having the slightest idea what to say or how this recent development is going to affect our plans.

Vance shuffles dejectedly across the floor and sits in the seat across from me. "Miranda, you don't think my band is stupid, do you?"

While I work on mending Vance's delicate ego, Kirsten makes calls. She calls everyone she knows who owns a car to see if they're willing to lend us theirs. Of course no one will, but you have to admire her persistence. Secretly, I'm not that disappointed. Vance has every right to sell his car if he wants. Besides, it wouldn't be so bad living in New York for a while.

After about an hour of telemarketing, Kirsten emerges with a new plan. "I know where we can get a car," she says, smiling. "My mom."

"That's great!" I had no idea that Kirsten had patched things up with her mother or even that she lived close by. "When did she say we could pick it up?"

"She doesn't know about it yet," Kirsten laughs.

Vance shakes his head. "You should at least call her first."

Kirsten throws her arms around Vance's neck and gives him an apologetic hug. "We'd just end up fighting over the phone and hanging up on each other. If I show up out of the blue we have to deal with each other face-to-face."

My gut tells me this isn't such a great idea, but it's not like I have much choice. Kirsten seems to know what she's doing, and I certainly don't have any better ideas.

She punches a number into the keypad of her cordless phone. "I'll find out when the next bus leaves for Cape May."

When Kirsten and I first talked about traveling the United States together, I thought we'd be tearing up the miles at lightning speed, putting as much distance between ourselves and Connecticut as we could. Maybe that will eventually happen, but right now we're at the Port Authority Bus Terminal waiting to board a poky New Jersey Transit bus that will get us to Cape May in four and a half hours. All this talk about traveling and I'm still not going to be any further than a day's ride from home.

"Just a couple of days—tops," Kirsten assures me in the main waiting room of the bus terminal. "All I need to do is convince my mom to let us borrow the old clunker that's been sitting in her garage for years, then we'll take it to a garage and get it fixed up."

Could it really be that easy? From the little I know about Kirsten's mother, I can't imagine she'd hand over her car just like that. The straps of my pack are digging into my shoulders, so I slide it off my back and set it down in the empty chair next to Vance. His face is pale and drawn, and he hasn't said two words since Kirsten called for the bus schedule. He's so crushed that she's leaving. I almost wonder if he made up that story about needing new drums just to keep Kirsten around for a few more days.

"What if she won't give it to us?" I ask.

"She will," Kirsten says with harsh determination in her eyes. "My mother has a lot of mistakes to make up for and she knows it. She wouldn't dare say no to me."

I don't like the way this sounds. It's like we're two bullies plotting to steal from some helpless old woman. I'm sure Kirsten's mom needs her car a lot more than we do—we can get along fine with buses and trains. But who knows what really went on between Kirsten and her mother. Maybe her mom really *did* do something terrible, something that's scarred Kirsten for life, something she needs to make up for. It *would* be nice to have wheels . . .

"They're boarding," Vance says sadly. "You might want to get on now so you can get a good seat." He takes Kirsten's bag for her and walks us out to the bus. I feel bad for him—he looks pretty wrecked. I know Kirsten just thinks of him as a friend, but Vance suddenly looks like someone in love.

Kirsten gives him a big, warm hug, and they rock together slowly for a moment or two like a dancing couple who hasn't noticed the music has ended. I stand off to the side, looking around at the people getting in line, trying not to see Vance's anguished face only a few feet away.

"Try to get those boxes and my bike in storage for me, would you?" Kirsten says, pulling away from Vance. Except for a tiny rasp in her voice she seems perfectly fine with saying good-bye. It hardly seems to bother her at all. "Hopefully the sublet will come through, and I won't have to pay this month's share of the rent."

Vance nods. Dark creases streak across his forehead, and his lips form a small, sad arch. "I'm really sorry about the car," he stammers. "I wasn't trying to—"

"It's okay," Kirsten hushes him. "I'm not mad or anything. It's all going to work out fine." She gives Vance a kiss on the bridge of his nose. "I'll write you, okay?"

Without saying a word, Vance's arms flop around her again, and he buries his face in Kirsten's neck. The bus is about three-quarters full, and there are at least ten people ahead of us. Not sure of what else to do, I get in line.

"Bye, Miranda," Vance says, waving, when Kirsten joins me.

I wave back. "Good luck with the band."

We board the bus, and I give Kirsten the window seat, but by the time we sit down Vance is already gone.

"I hope they show a movie," Kirsten says, her dry eyes fixated on the small TV monitor above our heads. Pressing a button on the armrest, she reclines the seat and closes her eyes. "Or maybe I'll just sleep the whole way."

When we make it through the other side of the tunnel into New Jersey, my eyes trace the fantastically jumbled skyline of New York City until it disappears behind a wall of leafy suburban trees. I've only been there two days and already I'm sad to go.

Kirsten keeps her eyes closed and never looks back. Not even once.

After two hours, the bus pulls into a rest stop just off the Garden State Parkway. Kirsten's been sleeping like a baby since Newark, while I've been wide awake stressing out over what's going to happen when we drop in on her mom unexpectedly. In my mind I see explosions of nuclear proportions, and me, caught somewhere at ground zero.

The young family sitting a few seats ahead of us stands up and inches down the aisle to the front of the bus. I gently nudge Kirsten's shoulder.

"Are we there?" she murmurs, her head flopping from one side to the other.

"Halfway," I say, stretching my legs.

The two elderly women sitting behind the driver are the only two people left on the bus besides me and Kirsten. They're both hopelessly hard-of-hearing but are very sweet and have spent the last two hours doing nothing but shouting at each other.

"DO YOU THINK WE'LL GET THERE

BEFORE IT GETS DARK?" the woman on the right says.

"I HOPE SO," answers the one on the left. "I WANT TO GO TO THE BEACH AS SOON AS WE GET THERE."

The elderly ladies' voices reverberate even louder now that the bus is empty, and I'm so glad because the noise finally wakes Kirsten up. When we get inside the rest stop pavilion, I talk her into buying a cup of coffee so I don't have to spend the rest of the trip bored out of my skull with no one to talk to.

"You're going to really like Cape May. This is the best time of year to go," Kirsten says as we stroll the souvenir shop, checking out the air-brushed sweatshirts and mugs with pictures of the Statue of Liberty. "You should know a few things before we get there, though. My mom isn't exactly the nicest person in the world, so if she tries to boss you around, don't let her get away with it. She's really opinionated, but you can just ignore it—she does it for show. It's probably a good idea to just let me do most of the talking."

I flip through the postcard rack, my head whirring with all these rules and conditions. What if I say something wrong and her mom gets mad? "You're sure we're doing the right thing?" I ask, my voice heavy with apprehension.

"Oh, yeah." Kirsten nods. "We need a car, right? Don't worry, I'll take care of it."

133

I know I should probably drop the subject, but I just can't. "What I mean is that if this is going to be so hard, maybe we shouldn't bother your mother at all. We can get by without a car, can't we? Why stir everything up?"

Kirsten gets this faraway look in her eyes, like she's someplace miles—or even years—from here. "Your family is still together, Miranda. You should be really grateful. My life's been turned upside down since the day my mom decided she didn't want to be married anymore, and I've always wanted her to know that. I want her to be sorry."

"She's not sorry?"

"Not enough," Kirsten answers flatly.

I lean against an old-fashioned machine that takes pennies and squeezes them flat, stamping them with a picture. I drop a new penny into the slot and turn the crank.

"When will it be enough?" I ask. The flattened penny comes out of the bottom, a smooth, shiny copper oval embossed with the Empire State Building. The faded image of Lincoln's head is hazy and warped in the background like a ghost. I give it to Kirsten.

"I don't know," she answers, rubbing the penny between her fingers. "Maybe never."

Well, what do you think?" Kirsten says as we stand on Beach Avenue, watching the bus pull away.

I fill my lungs with calming sea air. "It's beautiful," I answer. A fat seagull picks a stray French fry off the sidewalk, then waddles toward the beach with his loot. "When did you live here?"

"I didn't—Mom moved here when I was living with Dad," Kirsten says. "But I've visited a few times. The last time I was here was right after graduation." She picks up her pack and starts walking. "It's just a few streets over."

I follow Kirsten along the brick sidewalk into town, the tops of our heads warmed by the late afternoon sun. Cape May is definitely a resort town—I can tell by the number of ice-cream parlors, souvenir shops, and candy stores we pass within the first few minutes. For some reason, though, it's managed to escape some of the carnival tackiness you sometimes see in beach communities. There are literally dozens of old Victorian houses painted in soft pastel colors everywhere you look, most of them bed-and-breakfast places and guest houses, with big, wraparound porches and beautiful flowering bushes in the yard. They're all neat and cute like full-sized dollhouses. It's a giant contrast from Kirsten's stark walk-up on Tenth Street.

"It's sort of like Walt Disney World, isn't it?" Kirsten asks, practically reading my mind. "Everything's so perfect, it scares me." We walk a little further and turn onto Hughes Street. "There it is," she says. "That's my mom's place."

Kirsten points to a relatively modest two-story Victorian house the color of butter. The front porch is trimmed with lacy woodwork, and from the street I can see a matching gazebo in the backyard. A sign with fancy gold calligraphy hangs from a wrought-iron post at the end of the driveway that reads CAROLINE'S BED-AND-BREAKFAST.

"Caroline's my mom, in case you haven't figured that out," Kirsten jokes. I'd think Kirsten would be nervous to be here, but I can't tell. Her red lips are drawn into a thin, straight line, and her eyes refuse to let me in.

It probably won't be that bad, I tell myself, breathing in the heavy, sweet fragrance of the lilac bushes that border the property. *Even if Kirsten and her mom don't get along, I don't need to be in the middle of it. It's a big house. I can definitely find something to do on my own.*

136

"Should we go in, or do you want to wait until later?" I ask.

Kirsten hardens her jaw, her body stiffening defensively. "Let's go in right now. The sooner we get the car, the sooner we can get on the road. Maybe we'll even be able to leave tonight." With that, she marches up the porch steps with the staunch determination of a platoon sergeant.

Like a mouse, I shuffle in silently behind her, the sudden snap of the screen door announcing our arrival to the earthy, overfriendly woman behind the hospitality desk. She seems old enough to possibly be Kirsten's mother, with her brown bun and linen dress, but the generic way she's smiling at us tells me she's not.

"Welcome to Caroline's," the woman says mildly. "Do you have reservations?"

Kirsten rests her knuckles on the smooth oak counter. "Is Caroline here?" she asks gruffly.

The woman's smile shrinks. "Is there a problem?" she says, lowering her voice to just above a whisper, glancing nervously at the top of the stairs. "Something I could help you ladies with?"

"Yeah, we want to see Caroline," Kirsten says.

Kirsten can be so blunt sometimes, it makes me cringe inside.

"I see. . . . " The woman swallows a few times, then forces a smile. "And whom shall I say is asking?"

Kirsten doesn't even hesitate. "Tell Caroline her *daughter* is here to see her."

I smile weakly.

The woman clears her throat. "Oh . . . yes, of course—I'll be right back." She disappears through a doorway that leads to an elegant, formal dining room with a long mahogany table and sterling silver candlesticks. Kirsten flips through the guest book on the counter, turning the pages so hard, I'm sure they're going to rip. I stand back, looking at a small wall display holding pamphlets of local attractions. When the storm hits, I want to be safely out of the way.

"If she says no we're out of here," Kirsten informs me.

The sound of whispering voices echoes off the cream-colored walls, followed by footsteps making their way across the hardwood floor. I clutch the straps of my pack, waiting for the Dragon Lady to make her appearance.

"Kirsten! You really are here—I thought it was a prank!" Standing in the doorway is a short, slightly plump middle-aged woman in khaki pants and a denim shirt, with gently curled light blond hair framing her face. Standing side by side, she and Kirsten look so different, it seems impossible they come from the same gene pool. Where Kirsten's bone structure is sharp and defined, Caroline is more soft, with rounded edges. Kirsten gives off a relentless, in-your-face kind of energy, while Caroline seems gentle. The one trait they *do* share, though, is the same pretty slate-blue eyes.

138

Kirsten's mom wipes her hands on her kitchen apron and extends her fleshy arms for a hug. "You're here for a surprise visit! How wonderful!"

Arms at her side, Kirsten stiffens in her mother's embrace. "Actually, Mom, we're not going to stay. We just want to borrow your car."

Way to go, Kirsten, I think to myself, *So much for tact.* If I treated my mom like that—just rolling in after not seeing her for a year and demanding to use her car—she'd probably burst into hysterics.

Surprisingly, Caroline shrugs it off, seemingly happy that her daughter showed up at all, no matter what the reason. "Look how much your hair's grown in a year," she says, touching the ends. "Well, Kirsten, aren't you going to introduce me to your friend?"

"Right," Kirsten answers, as if she'd forgotten I was there. "Mom, this is Miranda. Miranda, Mom."

"I'm Caroline," she says, shaking my hand. "How do you do?"

"Fine, thanks," I answer with a nervous giggle. It's such a funny question—I'm never quite sure how to answer it. "You have a beautiful place here."

"Thank you." Caroline beams. "It's a lot of work, but it has many rewards." She looks at our backpacks. "There's an empty guest room on the right at the top of the stairs. Why don't you put your things in there for the time being and then you can join me in the library for tea."

"We don't have a lot of time—" Kirsten's face is stony, impenetrable. "We just came to find out about the car."

"Like I said, Kirsten," Caroline answers, flashing an uncompromising smile, "put your things upstairs and then we'll talk about it."

She always does this to me," Kirsten barks, hurling her pack onto one of the guest rooms' four-poster twin beds. The door is still open, and I wouldn't be surprised if her voice carried all the way down to the reception desk. "The second I walk in the door, she takes over, treating me like a kid."

There's so much I want to say to Kirsten, but I'm afraid she'll think I'm taking sides against her. I don't know what went on with her mom in the past, but what just happened seems more like a case of Kirsten acting like a baby than her mother treating her like one. I stand in front of the antique vanity mirror and distract myself with twirling my hair into a bun so I won't end up spilling my thoughts onto Kirsten.

Flopping down on the bed, she stares up at the ceiling. "She drives me crazy. It's like the minute I get anywhere near her, I become some helpless kid who can't say what's on her mind."

"You seemed to be doing a pretty good job to me," I say wryly.

"What's that supposed to mean?"

Playing with a few curls that frame my face, I avoid eye contact with her. "I mean, you told her right away we wanted to borrow the car. Isn't that what was on your mind?"

"I guess. I didn't want it to come out like that. . . ." Kirsten throws her arms over her head, kicks the side of the bed with her feet, and lets out a frustrated grunt. "I shouldn't have come here. Sometimes I think my life would be a lot simpler if I didn't have a mother."

I glance at the open door to see if Caroline's in the hall. Thankfully, no one's there.

"Ready for tea?" I say, tugging on Kirsten's foot.

"No . . ." Kirsten lowers her arms and looks at me. "How do you and your mom manage to get along so well?"

"What makes you think we get along?"

"You can just tell that sort of thing," Kirsten says. "You seem pretty comfortable around her."

I shrug. "Most of the time, I guess."

Kirsten sits up. "I'm never comfortable around mine."

Somehow I get the feeling Kirsten's exaggerating, but I don't call her on it. "Sometimes I think it helps to try to see your mom as a *person*—you know, with hopes, and feelings, and problems. . . ."

"Problems." Kirsten laughs dryly. "She's got oodles of those."

"Okay, don't focus on that—" I say. "Just try to remember there's more to your mom than someone who packed your school lunches and gave you a curfew. She has a life of her own."

Kirsten contemplates this for a moment, then looks up at me. "I have a better idea," she says. "Instead of having to think of my mom as a human being, why don't I just visit less often?"

The library is a sunny spot in the back of the house with a curved wall of windows overlooking the flower garden. Shelves of old leather-bound books run along the opposite wall, and I want more than anything to crack open a dusty old volume and sit on the window seat warming myself in rays of sunlight. Unfortunately, Kirsten and I have more pressing matters to deal with. Kirsten's mom is waiting for us at a table draped with white linens and a three-tiered silver serving dish.

"I had our cook brew a pot of vanilla tea—I know it's your favorite," Caroline says to Kirsten, pouring the tea through a silver strainer into each of our cups.

A man wearing glasses with black plastic frames walks into the library carrying a newspaper under his arm.

"That's Lionel," Caroline says to us. "He's my only guest right now. Tourist season won't really kick in until the Fourth of July." She turns to Lionel and waves. "Lionel, this is my daughter Kirsten and her friend Miranda."

Lionel smiles politely, then hides behind his newspaper.

During the introductions I check out the elegant morsels arranged on each tier. There are raspberry scones, little tea sandwiches without crusts, and tiny chocolate cream puffs and fruit tarts for dessert. I help myself to a cream cheese and cucumber sandwich.

"So what are you two up to with your backpacks?" Caroline says, passing me a bowl of sugar cubes. "Are you hiking through New Jersey?"

Kirsten laughs in spite of herself. "We're going cross-country," she says, regaining her sternness.

"For the summer?"

"For who knows how long," Kirsten says. "For how ever long we feel like."

I nibble as softly as a rabbit on my tea sandwich, wondering what Caroline's going to say. She might get mad, or maybe she'll ask a thousand questions, or maybe she'll cry—God knows my parents did all three.

Instead, Caroline's smile widens. "How exciting!" she says. "It sounds like quite an adventure."

Kirsten purses her lips and stares at her mother through slitted eyes. It's like she's mad at Caroline for saying that, which makes me want to grab Kirsten by the shoulders and shake her. Doesn't

145

she have any idea how lucky she is to have a mom who won't tie her down?

"Yeah, it's going to be great," Kirsten says pointedly, in a way that her mother seems to understand.

I take a sip of the aromatic tea. "Kirsten told me you've seen much of the country yourself," I say.

Caroline nods. The light seems to fade from her eyes. "I was a bit on the restless side—I couldn't stay in any place for too long."

"Or with *anyone* for too long," Kirsten adds with a touch of bitterness.

A burst of heat rises to my cheeks. I should've kept my mouth shut.

Caroline daintily dabs her mouth with a linen napkin, seemingly unfazed. "So is this why you want my car? To drive across the country?"

"You don't need it," Kirsten says. "That old Chevy's been rotting away in the garage for years."

"You mean the Nova?" Caroline says with a laugh. "I sold that thing last year. If I still had it, you'd be more than welcome to it, Kirsten. I'm sorry, but it's gone."

Kirsten stares down at her untouched cup of tea, which must be cold by now. I'm expecting her to suddenly demand the keys to the minivan parked in the driveway, but maybe she won't. Maybe even Kirsten realizes there's a limit to what she can expect of people.

"I guess there isn't anything else to talk about,

then," Kirsten says firmly, getting up from the table. "We'll just get our stuff and be on our way. . . . "

Just as Kirsten turns away, Caroline grabs her wrist. "Not so fast," she says darkly. "I haven't seen you in a year—you're not going to take off on me just like that. Stay for a day or two, or at least spend the night. You're not going to get very far before dark, and Miranda looks tired."

It seems abundantly clear that this is an order, not a request.

Caroline pats my hand, her softness returning. "You two can take as long as you want to figure out what you want to do."

"It *is* nice here . . . , " I say softly.

"Just tonight," Kirsten says, pulling her arm away. "And that's it."

It's Lionel's birthday, so that evening Caroline bakes a beautiful apple cake to celebrate. Lionel seems pleased, grinning content-edly at the candles while Caroline, Mary (the receptionist), and I sing "Happy Birthday." Kirsten claims she's too tired to come and stays up in the guest room the whole time.

"Anything else I can do?" Mary asks when Lionel retreats to his room with his third piece of apple cake.

Caroline shakes her head, balancing the glass cake stand in her hands. "Go on home. I'll see you tomorrow."

I collect the dirty plates and melted birthday candles and follow Caroline into the kitchen, which is as big as my parents' living room and as well-equipped as a restaurant. "The cake was great," I say, dumping the dishes in the big alu-minum sink.

Caroline smiles, touching the knobs on the big gas oven to make sure they're all off. "It's so quiet—it's hard to believe this place is going to be filled to the gills with guests and staff. I'm not quite ready for it yet."

I sit on a stool and watch Caroline wrap the remainder of the cake in big sheets of waxed paper. Through the screen door I hear crickets chirping lazily in the cool, dark garden—they aren't in a hurry to go anywhere, and neither am I. New York made me feel like I always had to be doing something, like I was running some invisible race with myself, but here I'm content to sit on this stool and feel the ocean air trickle in through the window screens, watching Caroline wrap apple cake forever.

"You like what you do," I observe.

"It's my life," Caroline says simply. "The house is great, and I'm surrounded by good people for most of the year, so I'm rarely lonely—although I do miss my daughter. I wish she'd come by more often." She puts the cake away in the closet-sized refrigerator. "I love running this place. I feel like it's what I was meant to do."

"How do you know?" I ask. "I can't decide what to do tomorrow, let alone what I'm supposed to do for the rest of my life."

Caroline wipes up the counter with a big yellow sponge. "You'll know when you find it. It'll just *feel* right. It'll fill this space in your heart where you didn't even know there was a hole," she says. "It took me a long time to figure it out, though. I did a lot of searching—I'm sure Kirsten's already filled you in."

I shake my head. "Not really."

"Basically, I woke up one day and realized I was still young but hadn't really done anything for myself. I had a kid, and a husband who I no longer felt connected to, and the idea of spending the rest of my life in the same house, living in the same town . . . well, it really scared me."

I nod sympathetically, but I can't really understand. My mother gave up a lot to raise Jayson, Abigail, and me, and *she* didn't run away. Moms are supposed to tough it out, right? Isn't that their job?

"I know Kirsten still blames me for divorcing her father," Caroline continues. She stares out the window, her eyes distant. "I can't seem to make her understand that it was something I had to do at the time. I was going crazy. But I'll tell you something—if I had known it was going to ruin my relationship with my daughter, I wouldn't have done it."

Why is she telling me all this? Kirsten should be the one sitting on the stool, listening to the story—not me. Maybe Caroline's hoping I'll pass some of this on to Kirsten so she won't have to do it herself. But that's not going to happen. This is one battle I really don't want to be dragged into.

"Why don't you tell this to Kirsten?" I gently

suggest. "Maybe it'll help her understand."

"I've tried, but it's impossible to get through to her—she won't let me in at all. I've given up trying to reach her. Now I just leave her alone to come to me whenever she feels like it. I'll take whatever I can get."

Even though I'm not tired, I stretch my arms over my head and yawn. "I think I'm going to take a bath," I say, glancing at the schoolhouse clock on the wall. "After we hit the road tomorrow, who knows when we'll have the luxury of hot water again."

"The linen closet's in the hall. You'll find some fresh towels and some bath salts in there," Caroline says.

"Thanks."

"Miranda, before you go, could you do me a favor?"

"Sure."

Tiny creases form around Caroline's frowning mouth. "If there's any way you can convince Kirsten to stay—even for one more day—I'd really appreciate it. I'd ask her myself, but you know how bad she responds to me. It's been a year since I've seen her, and I'm afraid of how long it might be until the next time."

The request weighs heavily on my shoulders. I try to think of some way to get out of it, but Caroline's pleading eyes are wearing on my conscience. "I'll see what I can do."

"Thank you so much," she says, patting my arm. "I'm so sorry if this puts a damper on your plans."

"It's okay," I say, getting up to leave. "We don't have any."

After my long soak in the big porcelain bathtub, I wrap myself in the thick, white guest robe and make my way down to the first floor, all sweet-smelling and relaxed, my mind set on exploring the library. First, though, I take a quick detour, ducking into the doorless closet near the front desk and dial up a number on the pay phone.

"Hello?" says the bright young voice on the other line.

"Abigail . . . it's me."

"Miranda? Oh, my God!" she squeals. "Where are you? You must be in Oklahoma by now!"

"Don't get carried away—it's only been a couple of days." I laugh. "Actually, I'm in New Jersey."

"Jersey?"

"Kirsten's mom lives here," I quickly explain, almost apologizing. "We're in Cape May, all the way at the bottom of the state. I haven't had much time to go exploring, but it's really nice around here. It's on the shore. . . . "

"I'm trying to picture it, but it's pretty hard without a postcard to look at."

I roll my eyes. "I'm working on it, okay? Let me get off the East Coast first."

"I didn't get any mail this morning, and it ruined my whole day." Even though I can't see her face, I know Abigail is pouting at me right now.

"I'm sure you'll live," I say. "So what's new?"

"Nothing much. Mom and Dad have been moping around. Mom cried the whole way home after we dropped you off."

I'm not sure why, but for some reason this makes me smile a little. "Put them on, will you?"

"They're not home—they went out to dinner with the Bartletts. They said they'd be home around ten," Abigail says.

My heart sinks. "That's all right," I say, trying not to sound disappointed. "I don't really have anything to tell, anyway. I just wanted to say hi."

"Hi," Abigail jokes.

"Hi," I joke back. "Is there anything else new?"

"Let's see . . ." The line is silent for a moment. "We had chicken for dinner last night."

"I'm sorry I missed all that excitement," I tease.

"No you're not."

The line goes quiet again. I wish I had something else to say, but my mind is blank. "I guess I'll go, then. Make sure you tell Mom and Dad I called."

"I will. Don't forget the postcards."

"I won't," I say. "Bye."

"Bye, Miranda."

I wait for Abigail to hang up first.

It's late when I tiptoe back to our guest room. I slide in between the crisp sheets, listening to Kirsten breathing heavily in the bed next to mine. Even though my head feels weighty against the soft feather pillow, I'm restless, thinking about how I'm supposed to keep Kirsten from leaving tomorrow. I'm not sure exactly how I got involved in this sticky situation, but since Caroline was kind enough to feed me and let me stay here, I figure I owe it to her to give it a shot.

Kirsten tosses fitfully in her bed. "Miranda? Are you awake?" I hear her groggy voice cutting through the darkness.

"Yeah," I answer, turning over.

"I know you wanted to head as far west as we could, but we should go somewhere fairly close by, so we don't have to spend days at a time on a bus. I was thinking maybe Philadelphia, or visiting your brother in Virginia."

"I'm up for anything," I answer. "But you know, Kirsten, I kind of like it here. This is my first time at Cape May, and I wouldn't mind hanging out here for a few days—you know, before we head out."

Kirsten falls silent. I open my eyes, watching the moonlight cast its white glow on the floor, wondering if Kirsten is detecting a note of insincerity in my voice.

"We can't stay," Kirsten says firmly. "I'm sure my mom wants us out of here before the guests arrive."

"They won't be here for a few more days," I argue. "Besides, I think your mom misses having you around."

As my eyes adjust to the darkness, I see the black outline of Kirsten's body suddenly sit up in bed. "Is that what she said?"

Tread carefully, I tell myself. *You don't want Kirsten to think her mother put you up to this.* "Not in so many words," I say. "When we first got here she was so happy to see you. It's obvious that she loves you."

"Yeah, right."

"I mean it. I don't know what happened between you two, but I think she really wants to make it up to you."

Kirsten exhales. I can almost feel the tension draining out of her with each breath. "Sometimes I think she does, but . . . "

"But what?"

"But I don't know if I can trust her," Kirsten

157

whispers. "A lot of stuff happened, Miranda. You don't even know. . . . "

I'm afraid to ask what she means, but many wild explanations run through my head, terrible things I couldn't imagine someone as sweet and as nice as Caroline doing. I want to believe Kirsten, but I keep thinking that maybe her memories are just blowing everything out of proportion.

"There were a lot of promises she didn't keep," Kirsten says vaguely. "She made a lot of mistakes."

"She seems like she has her life together now, though, doesn't she?" I say gently. "She might not be the same person you remember."

"Maybe not," Kirsten admits. "It's hard to tell."

I don't even know what I'm talking about anymore—my mouth has sort of taken over, making me argue for something I know nothing about. "Kirsten, can I ask you a question?"

"Sure."

"Why did you stop visiting your mom when you moved to your dad's in Connecticut?" I ask.

There's a pause. I can hear her sliding under the covers again. "We had a big blowout."

"About what?"

"You know," Kirsten says with a weak laugh, "I don't even remember."

The next morning, before Kirsten wakes up, I throw on my racer-back swimsuit, a pair of shorts, and a T-shirt and head for the beach. I leave a note on her pillow telling her I'll be gone for the day, but I don't tell her where I'm going or when I'll be back. I'm hoping it'll give Kirsten and Caroline some time alone to talk things out so we can finally get on the road.

Late in the afternoon, when I've maxed out on sand and surf, Kirsten's waiting for me on the porch swing, bare toes kicking the air as I walk up to the house. The sun has already begun to dip behind the sprawling mint-green inn across the street, spiking the smooth blue sky with clouds the color of sherbet. It's like being in a town where everything is made of candy. As I skip up the steps to the house, I fantasize about breaking off a piece of the buttery porch railing and letting it melt on my tongue like toffee.

"It's about time! I thought I was going to have to send out a search party!" Kirsten says, wiggling her long toes at me. "Where were you?"

"The beach," I say with a lazy grin. My muscles feel as loose as rubber bands, and my skin smells like salt.

"Thanks for leaving me behind."

I slump beside her on the swing. "I thought you might need some time alone with your mom. I didn't want to get in the way."

"Please," Kirsten says ruefully. "We could've used you as a referee."

"That bad?"

"Well, no, it wasn't *that* bad, but we did have it out, as usual. She was bugging me about quitting my job and 'roaming around' as she so aptly puts it."

From inside the house, sounds of footsteps and creaking furniture filter through the screen door, mingling with waves of cooking smells. I can't see who's moving around the entrance of the house, but I have no doubt they can hear every word we're saying. Lionel, who's reading the paper at the opposite end of the porch, has his head slightly cocked to one side as if he's tuning in, too.

"So what did you say?" I answer, dropping my volume discreetly.

"I told her she was a hypocrite," Kirsten says, her voice a little louder and a little clearer than before, making sure every member of her audience hears it. I swear I can see Lionel's ears twitching. "There's no way she's going to tell me what to do when she did the exact same thing herself. So I went upstairs and started getting our stuff together—I was going to go find you so we could take off—but she followed me and said she was sorry for what she'd said. Then she told me she knew where we could get a car."

I give the swing a push with my sandy feet. "You're kidding!"

"There's a friend of hers who lives a few streets over who wants to get rid of her old Ford Escort. It's pretty rusty and needs a few things but she said she'd sell it to us for eight hundred dollars if we wanted it."

"I don't know, Kirsten," I say doubtfully. "Four hundred bucks apiece is a lot of money, and the car might be a dud. My cash has to last me awhile."

"It won't be four hundred dollars each," Kirsten says, smiling. "Mom actually offered to pay for half! She likes to pull a grand gesture like this whenever I'm mad at her."

"Two hundred bucks . . . " It sounds like a pretty good deal, and I could probably swing it, but I've got this gnawing feeling in my gut that we could be making a big mistake.

Kirsten's eyes are wide with possibility. "It's only two hundred apiece, plus we'll split the bill for the tune-up and whatever else it needs."

"How much is that going to come to?" I ask warily.

"It can't be *that* much." Kirsten shrugs. "Just

think, Miranda, soon we'll be able to head west just like you wanted. I've been doing some reading about cattle ranches in Montana. We could be there two weeks from now, herding baby cattle alongside cute cowboys in tight jeans, under the open sky," she says dreamily. "Unless you want to hop a train and go to Pennsylvania instead. I hear there are some killer parties in Amish country this time of year."

I'm trying to be sensible about this and think it through like an adult, but Kirsten's got me caving in already before I even know all the facts. She's annoyingly persuasive. I see little hope of getting out of this one, even if I wanted to.

"*If* I agree to buy the car with you, how long would it take to get it fixed?" I ask.

A triumphant light glows from behind Kirsten's eyes. She knows she's got me. "The mechanic said that if there aren't any major problems it'll be ready by the end of the week, maybe even sooner. In fact, he was able to squeeze in an oil change today."

I stop the swing. "He's working on the car already?"

"Well, yeah," Kirsten says, looking at me like I'm a moron. "Don't you want to leave as soon as possible?"

I shake my head, totally confused. "But we didn't even buy the car yet!"

Kirsten gets the swing rocking again. "Sure we

did. Mom and I went to pick it up this afternoon."

Staring hard at her, I'm totally amazed and completely irritated by her sheer audacity. "You should've asked me first. . . . "

"You took off and didn't tell me where you were," Kirsten rationalizes. "What was I supposed to do? We need a car, don't we? If I'd waited until you came home, someone could've bought the car already. I had to make an executive decision."

What can I say? She does have a point. "What if you'd bought it, though, and I'd ended up saying no?"

"Come on, Miranda." Kirsten narrows her eyes and shakes her head like I'm being ridiculous. "We're road buddies now—I knew you wouldn't let me down."

After dinner, Kirsten and I help Caroline out with the dishes. Believe it or not, it's Kirsten's idea. She scrubs the pots and pans in the big aluminum sink while I dry and Caroline puts away. The tension between the two of them seems to have lessened considerably, if not temporarily, and it's no mystery that the car is playing a major role in the bonding process. It's interesting to watch their little mother-daughter game unfold. For Kirsten, getting her mom to buy half the car is a victory, a payback of part of the emotional debt she feels she's due. For Caroline, I get the feeling that owning half of Kirsten's car is a way for her to keep some semblance of control over her daughter. I wish the two of them would just forgive each other and get on with their own lives.

When we're done with the dishes, Kirsten and I borrow Caroline's minivan to go see a movie at the multiplex a few towns over. We don't have a clue what the movie's supposed to be about other than it's the first summer blockbuster action movie of the year, which means enough explosions and car chases and silly one-liners to make us completely escape reality for an hour and a half. I'm still full from dinner, but Kirsten buys a big tub of popcorn and dumps a big box of Milk Duds in it, making a big, sticky, chocolatey mess.

"Which movie won the Academy Award for Best Picture in 1953?" Kirsten's reading aloud the trivia questions they show on the screen before the movie starts. I slump down in my seat, resting my right ankle on my left knee, and pick out the few kernels in Kirsten's popcorn bucket that aren't coated in goo.

"That was my second guess!" Kirsten groans, reading the answer on the screen.

Out of the corner of my eye I catch two figures walking down the aisle. It's two guys who look like brothers—one is about my age, the other looks like he's a few years younger. The guy who's my age has light brown chin-length hair that keeps falling in his eyes. *I love hair like that.* Every time he runs his fingers through it, I catch a heart-stopping glimpse of his tanned skin and pouty lips.

They sit across the aisle from us.

I nudge Kirsten's arm. "Did you see that guy?" I'm practically mouthing the words to her so they won't hear me. "*So* cute!"

Instead of slyly turning around and catching a quick glance of him while pretending to look at the door, Kirsten turns her head and looks at them straight on. "Kids," she says bluntly.

I'm cringing so hard, I think my skull is going to collapse. "He's *our* age," I say, using the popcorn tub as soundproofing material. "You call that too young?"

"You should always date someone older than you," she answers matter-of-factly.

"How old?"

Kirsten ponders the question for a moment. "By at least thirty years, maybe even forty," she deadpans.

I burst out laughing louder than I mean to, and on the edge of my field of vision I see Cute Guy's head turn toward me. I cower even more in my seat, jabbing Kirsten in the ribs. "He's looking at us."

Kirsten turns her head at looks back. "Of course he's looking at us; we're the best-looking women in here."

Impulsively, I touch my face checking for chocolate, then smooth down my hair and sit up straight, crossing my legs as gracefully as the cramped seat will allow. I toss a popcorn kernel casually into my mouth and stare intently at the trivia questions on the screen, just in case Cute Guy happens to be glancing my way.

"You're pathetic," Kirsten teases.

I giggle sheepishly. "I know."

Kirsten licks a bit of caramel off her fingers. "I

never did ask you what happened with Rick that night at The Chiller. It looked like he was making some serious moves on you."

"He *would* have if you hadn't spoiled it," I say lightly, only half-joking.

"I told you, Rick can really be a bad boy sometimes." Kirsten tilts her head back and tosses a piece of popcorn in her mouth. "He zeroed in on you like a heat-seeking missile."

"It wasn't like that—or so I thought," I answer, my cheeks growing warm. "We had a lot in common. We were having a good conversation. The club was hot, and he wanted some fresh air, and he asked me to keep him company."

"Some guy you hardly know asks you to step outside and you just go like that?"

"He's *your* friend," I argue. "I figured he had to be all right."

"My friends are the ones you *especially* have to watch out for," Kirsten says, shaking her head. "You've never had a serious boyfriend, have you?"

I hide my face behind the tub of popcorn. "Does it show that much?"

"You seem a little young around guys."

"And I suppose you've had tons of experience?" I answer defensively.

"Not a lot, but some . . . " A secret smile crosses Kirsten's face. "You've got to learn how to play the game a little."

"I don't believe in playing games."

Kirsten raises her dark eyebrows. "That's half your problem."

Staring at the screen, I think back on the few brief romantic encounters I've had: the guy I met at a party who said he liked me but didn't want a long-distance relationship even though he only lived fifteen minutes away; the few group dates Chloe had set up that seemed to fizzle before they even started; and of course the infamous prom date who spent the whole evening trying to crawl down the front of my dress, later spreading rumors that I couldn't keep my hands off him. All in all, I'd say my love life has been almost a complete disaster, but I don't see how playing games could've made it any better.

I lean my head against the back of the seat. "Have you ever been in love?"

"Twice." Kirsten stares past me, seemingly lost in thought. "When I was fifteen on summer vacations with my dad in Canada I met this guy named Marc. It was a nice summer thing, but it didn't last, for obvious reasons. The other guy I met when I was seventeen."

"Someone from Greenwich?" I ask hopefully.

Kirsten nods.

I turn and stare into her face. "Do I know him?"

"Maybe," she says coyly, picking a corn kernel off her shorts.

"You have to tell me!"

Kirsten shakes her head. "I can't—really."

168

"Can I guess? At least let me guess!"

"You can guess all you want, but I won't tell you if you're right," Kirsten answers stubbornly.

Curiosity is burning inside of me, but no amount of prodding will get Kirsten to give up any details. "If you're not going to name names, then at least tell me what happened . . . *please*," I beg.

"If you *must* know, he broke up with me," Kirsten says. "We weren't exactly a well-matched couple; in fact, we were total opposites. But we did have this amazing attraction between us. I thought it made things interesting. He thought it made things too complicated."

"Jerk!"

Kirsten snickers. "He wasn't a jerk; he was just a little too realistic. Anyway, he was right—it wouldn't have worked out in the end. It still hurts every once in a while, when I think about it, creeping up on me when I least expect it."

I don't know what to say, so I don't say anything at all. Kirsten seems swept away by her own thoughts, making me wonder if maybe she's still in love with this mystery man.

A moment later Kirsten snaps out of her daze, her face suddenly brightening. "You know, Miranda, I'm so glad we're going on the road together," she says. "You're a lot of fun to be with."

"I am?"

Kirsten laughs. "You sound surprised."

I shrug. "Sometimes it's hard to know what other people really think of you."

"You think too much," she says. "Just say *thanks*."

"All right," I say, laughing. "Thanks."

The next few days pass by like a whirlwind. With tourist season fast approaching, there is much to be done around the house before the guests arrived. Kirsten and I help Caroline and Mary carefully fold sets of cotton sheets and towels, polish silverware, and make tiny guest baskets of shampoo and lavender-scented soap. There is dusting and polishing of furniture, painting of trim to be done on the gazebo, and bushes to be pruned in the backyard. Max, the cook, arrives with tons of new recipes, and we get to try them all. It's good to be so busy. Every day flies by, and every night I sleep soundly, knowing that as soon as our car is ready, Kirsten and I will be free of obstacles and can finally leave.

In between the busy preparations, I still find time to sneak out of the house by myself so Kirsten and her mom have time to be alone and talk about things. Twice I rent a bike at the Village Bike Shop and cruise up and down Beach Avenue and around town, eating hot funnel cakes and checking out the little gift shops downtown. Another day I visit the Cape May Point lighthouse and climb the 199 steps to the top. The air is clear and crisp, giving a perfect view of Delaware Bay and the peninsula that goes on for miles and miles. The visitor's guide says that when the lighthouse was built in 1859, the beacon was lit by oil lamps and the light was magnified by prisms and lenses. As I lean against the railing and stare out at the little pockets of golden sunlight settling in the troughs of the waves, I imagine myself a hundred years ago in a long Victorian gown, climbing the spiral staircase at dusk to light the beacon that will cut through the night fog and guide sailors to safety. I mention this to Abigail on the back of the postcard I buy for her. It shows a dark silhouette of the lighthouse against an orange sunset.

There are lots of nature trails in the park surrounding the lighthouse, and I wind my way through them on foot, stopping at the observation platforms to take in the scenery. The trails are lush with bushes and plants and small wildflowers in varying shades of yellow and white and pink. I can't name any of them, but I know Mom could if she were here. I wonder what she's doing right at this very minute. Is she worrying about me like she said she would, or has her life continued on like normal and she's too busy to even think about me?

Speaking of moms, I've started to notice that

Kirsten has grown a lot closer to Caroline over the last few days. Working together in the house must be helping. Kirsten is less confrontational and actually looks her mother in the eye now when she talks to her, and Caroline has stopped walking on eggshells around Kirsten. They laugh a lot, too. Once, when we were tying up some flowers in the pantry to be dried for potpourri, they start joking about some of Kirsten's dad's quirky habits. I got the sense this is usually a sore subject. It's nice to see them making some progress.

The next day the summer tourist season begins with full force. The Martins, a young honeymooning couple visiting from Chicago, arrive early in the afternoon. Mrs. Martin (which she insists we call her, even though she can't be more than four years older than Kirsten) is dressed in pearls and a canary-yellow tailored suit and has five pieces of heavy luggage we have to carry upstairs for her. She's easily excitable and has this terrible habit of gasping every time she sees something new, then saying how cute or quaint it is. It takes me a while to get used to being around her. Every two minutes she makes me jump, thinking she's about to have a heart attack.

Gasp. "John! Did you see the banister? Isn't it absolutely adorable?"

Gasp. "John! You didn't forget to buy film, did you, darling?"

Gasp. "John! Have you seen the view outside

173

our window!" *Gasp. Gasp.* "Isn't this house marvelous? It's so quaint!"

I'm tempted to give Mrs. Martin a paper bag so she won't hyperventilate.

Mrs. Martin's husband, John, looks a few years older than his new wife and seems exceptionally patient with her. He's wearing expensive-looking trousers and a nice dress shirt that's wrinkled at the elbows, probably from Mrs. Martin tugging him in all directions to show him quaint things. John smiles mildly whenever she gasps and rubs her shoulders, or gives her a peck on the cheek.

The other guests are an adorable family from Wilkes-Barre, Pennsylvania. They have the biggest room in the house, overlooking the garden out back. The Pearsons are casual, down-to-earth people, unlike the stuffy Martins, and they have a two-year-old son named Kyle who has a head of golden curls that make him look like an angel. Behind the cherubic face, though, is a mischievous little devil of the highest order. Barbara, his mom, told me about the one time she left Kyle for a minute to hang some clothes outside. While she was gone he somehow managed to crawl out of his playpen, lock the door, then turn on all the burners on the stove. It took the help of neighbors and several members of the Wilkes-Barre Fire Department to get Barbara back inside the locked house before little Kyle had a chance to torch the place.

In addition to the Martins and the Pearsons,

Lionel's still here, which means all the bedrooms are full if you count the one Kirsten and I are sharing. Luckily, the couple who reserved our room won't be here for another day. Our car should be ready by then, so everything should work out perfectly.

An hour before dinner I wander around the house restlessly, hoping to catch a minute with Kirsten. We've hardly had a chance to talk at all since the guests started arriving—she's been way to busy helping her mom with all the details. I keep offering to give her a hand, but Kirsten refuses, saying she wants to do it herself.

By sheer luck I run into her on the stairs, black wisps of hair flying all around her face.

"What are you doing?" I ask, stepping aside as she sails by me to the front door.

Kirsten shoves a wad of money in her front pocket. "Mrs. Martin is wondering where her 'Honeymoon Basket' is—Mom wants me to throw something together."

"Do you want me to come?"

"Nah. It won't take me long." Kirsten dashes outside, the screen door slapping behind her.

My stomach growls as the aroma of the chicken that Max has been roasting all afternoon slowly wafts up the stairs. I groan. When you're hungry, the hour before dinnertime can seem like the longest hour of the day. To take my mind off my stomach, I dig out Kirsten's atlas and my guidebook and trace different routes we can take. Interstate 80 might be a good bet—it'll take us through Pennsylvania, Ohio, Indiana; then it grazes Chicago at the bottom of Lake Michigan and shoots off toward the Plains states, Iowa, Nebraska, cutting through Wyoming, clipping off the notch in Utah, through Nevada, and finally ending in San Francisco. Or we could follow 80 until Chicago, then get on either 90 or 94 through Minnesota, the Dakotas, Montana, the very tip of Idaho, ending up in Seattle, Washington. From there we could go south to San Francisco. Or maybe we should skip the interstates altogether and just travel the two-lane roads so we don't miss the scenery.

As my fingers work their way along the spidery network of highways, cities, towns, and bridges, over miles and miles of rivers and lakes and parks and mountains, I feel the travel bug burning in my blood. It wasn't so long ago that I was in the car with my parents, on the way to New York, afraid I had made a terrible mistake. But now, after getting the tiniest glimpse of what's waiting for me out there, I want to get moving. I'm anxious to feel the miles spinning out from underneath me, not knowing what's going to happen or who I'm going to meet next. I'm tired of being young and inexperienced—it's time to see what real life is all about.

Kirsten comes back with a straw basket and a

brown grocery bag. She hardly gives me a second glance as she dumps everything onto her bed and starts winding a silky yellow ribbon around the handle of the basket.

"Kirsten," I say, swinging my legs over the other side of the bed so I can show her the map. "I have a few ideas about routes. . . ."

"Can we talk about it later?" she interrupts, trying to arrange a bottle of champagne, some French cheese, crackers, and caviar in the basket.

"Okay . . . " I skulk back to my side of the room and quietly work on a hangnail that's been bugging me all day.

"I didn't mean to snap," Kirsten apologizes. "I just want to get this to *Mrs.* Martin before she has a fit."

"That's cool," I say, not looking up.

Kirsten tosses me a gold foil-covered truffle. "We'll talk about it later, okay?"

I set the chocolate on the nightstand next to my bed. "Sure," I say, "Whatever."

n celebration of the arrival of the first guests of the season, tonight's dinner is especially festive. The dining room table has been pulled out to its maximum length and is dressed with fine linen, candles, a vase of lilacs, and the silverware Kirsten and I spent an afternoon laboriously polishing. It all looks so perfect, I'm afraid to touch anything.

Everyone's at the table ready to eat at seven o'clock on the dot, except for the Martins, who float down the stairs fifteen minutes late. Even Lionel, who rarely joins us at dinner, comes to the table looking scrubbed with his thinning wet hair parted to one side. Caroline and Kirsten sit at the ends of the table, and the rest of us fill in the middle, with me sitting directly across from Kyle's high chair.

The door to the kitchen swings open, and Max comes out in his chef's uniform, carrying a silver platter of carved chicken. A gasping sound erupts to the right of me. "John! Look at the chicken!

Have you ever seen anything so gorgeous in your life?"

Kirsten and I exchange subtle but definitely amused looks.

Lionel appears visibly shaken by Mrs. Martin's outburst. He rubs his hands together nervously, looking at the kitchen, then the stairs, then the kitchen again, as if trying to decide if he should make a run for it and have his dinner up in his room like he usually does, or stick around for the sake of politeness.

"You like chicken, don't you, Kyle?" Barbara Pearson says, moving one of the candles the toddler's reaching for. Kyle gives his mom a gurgly nod and shoves a wad of tablecloth into his angelic mouth.

"What an adorable little boy you have!" Mrs. Martin gasps. "He's darling!"

"Thank you," Barbara says, smiling warmly.

James Pearson beams with pride at his son. "He's at the age now that we have to watch him every second."

Mrs. Martin wiggles her nose playfully at little Kyle. "John, I want a baby just like this adorable little creature right here."

"Whatever you want, darling," John says, rubbing her shoulder.

Kirsten holds a napkin in front of her face and slyly makes a retching face at me like she's going to be sick. I quickly take a gulp of ice water to keep from laughing. The look in Kirsten's eyes tells me she's thinking of the same thing I am—Mrs. Martin in her canary-yellow suit having to crawl through a window because her adorable little creature locked her out. I'd pay a million bucks to see that.

No one says much of anything as we pass around the serving dishes. Lionel nearly drops the basket of rolls when Mrs. Martin gasps at the sight of baby carrots, and Kyle grabs a fistful of chicken and throws it into Mrs. Martin's water glass, but other than that, the meal is pretty uneventful. The food is delicious, and I try to savor every bite, knowing that once we're on the road we'll probably be eating a lot of junk food. Who knows when we'll be having a home-cooked meal again?

Kirsten hasn't said much to me during dinner, and I'm starting to wonder if I said something to make her mad. Was it because I bugged her when she was making up the basket? Nah. She's not the type to hold a grudge over something so small. It seems like it's been days since we've had a decent conversation—the movie theater was the last time we really spoke to one another about something that didn't involve the inn. Maybe I'm just being oversensitive, but sometimes I swear it seems as though Kirsten forgets that I'm even here.

When dinner's over, Lionel says a quick thank-you to Caroline, then bolts upstairs. No one lingers over coffee; they just get up and leave. I stick around to help Caroline and Kirsten clear the table.

"Did the garage call?" I ask, partly because I'm curious and partly to remind Kirsten I'm still around. "Is the car going to be ready soon?"

Caroline looks up from the dishes she's stacking in the dishwasher rack and flashes Kirsten and me this strange look. I'm not exactly sure what to make of it.

Kirsten scrapes the plates into the garbage, avoiding her mother's gaze. "I haven't heard anything," she answers, shrugging her shoulders.

"Maybe we should give them a call," I suggest. "When the guests get here we won't have anywhere to go."

Kirsten doesn't answer. *Okay, what did I say?* A guilty weight settles in the middle of my chest.

"I'm sorry . . . ," I blurt out stupidly, not even knowing what I'm supposed to be sorry for. *Would someone please tell me what I'm doing wrong?*

Caroline steps toward me and smiles awkwardly, brushing a few curls off my shoulder in a motherly way. "You have such nice hair, Miranda. I've always wanted hair like yours."

There's something in her touch—a gentle undercurrent—that tells me I should leave them alone to talk. *Fine with me,* I think, wiping my hands on a dish towel. *This is getting too weird.*

"I'll be upstairs," I say.

Kirsten smiles vaguely, her blue eyes slipping right past me.

Back in the room, I bury my face in the pillow on my bed, breathing in the cool scent of lace, hoping it will ease the pressure that's building in my rib cage. Absently, I flip through the travel book Dad gave me, waiting for Kirsten to get back. I wait . . . and wait . . . and wait. It feels like hours have passed since dinner. The house is so quiet, it's almost like everyone has left. I have this bizarre image in my head of everyone waiting for me to lock myself in my room and, when the coast is clear, they tiptoe out of the house and all go on the road together without me. *"Phew, that was a close one!"* I can picture Kirsten saying behind the wheel of our Escort with the Martins, the Pearsons, Lionel, and Caroline all crammed in the back. *"Can you believe it? She actually thought she was going with us!"*

Despite my paranoid delusions of Kirsten taking off without me, the door to the room creaks open and she waltzes in, the corners of her mouth twitching secretively. She turns down her bed like a maid in a hotel and starts to undress without saying a word. Kirsten doesn't elaborate on what she was talking about with her mother, and I don't dare ask. I'd really love to find out if I've done anything to upset her, but an inner voice holds me back. Now is not the time.

182

"It's probably too late to think about the trip, huh?" I ask hesitantly.

"Yeah." Kirsten sighs, slipping on an oversized blue T-shirt. "I'm really tired."

I close the book and toss it on the floor. It makes a loud slapping sound when it hits.

"My mom had this great idea," Kirsten suddenly says as she slides into bed. "There's a ferry that goes across the bay to Delaware. It takes about an hour. We should check it out tomorrow."

"Fine," I say, though it's clear we're going, anyway, regardless of what I think. A sharp, cold ball slowly turns inside my torso. Picking the book off the floor, I roll over to one side and pull my knees to my chest and start to read.

Kirsten turns off the light.

"Good night, Miranda," she says.

I stare into the blackness. "Good night."

can't remember the last time I went on a ferry," I say to Kirsten as we begin to board the big white vessel called the *Cape Henlopen*. The ferry is much bigger than I thought it would be—it kind of looks like a cruise ship. Hundreds of people are pouring onto the boat, and there's a long line of cars waiting to drive up onto the lower deck.

Kirsten still isn't saying much and she hardly answers me when I ask her if she'd rather sit inside or outside. The silence is getting pretty aggravating. I'm getting so I don't even want to ask questions anymore because I'm tired of being ignored. I hope it's not going to be like this when we're on the road. If that's the case, I'd rather be alone.

It's a beautiful day, so I decide to stay outside, staking out a spot near the back of the ferry on the upper deck, where you can watch the cars roll on one by one. Kirsten follows without saying a word.

"I don't know why it's so cool to see a car on

a boat, but it is," I say lightly as a strong gust of wind blows a strand of hair into my mouth. I brush it away. "It makes me wish the Escort was ready. It would've been fun to bring it."

"Hmmm . . . ." Kirsten closes her eyes and tilts her face up toward the midmorning sun.

Behind us, a family of six sits on one of the wooden benches. The father, a tall man with a big round belly and a booming voice, threatens to take the youngest inside the boat if he doesn't stop squirming. Below, the last car pulls up and the gate closes behind it. There is the deep groan of scraping metal and a sudden jolt as we pull away from the dock. I clutch the railing, steadying myself as the deck pitches and rolls underfoot.

Kirsten leans over the railing, rocking in whichever direction the boat takes her. Her eyes are dark and brooding, even more than they were last night. I watch the lacy white foam splash against the side of the ferry as it cuts a sharp arc away from Cape May, my heart beating with a certain, unnamed dread.

I can't stand it anymore. I have to say something. "Kirsten?" The engine grows louder as we approach full speed. The warmth of the sun on my bare arms is wiped away by the wind. Goose bumps prickle my skin. "Did I do or say something to make you mad?"

Kirsten suddenly turns to me, looking confused. "Huh?"

"From the way you've been acting, I feel like I must've said or done something wrong. I have no idea what I did, so if you'd just tell me . . . "

"You didn't do anything," she says, shaking her head. Then, turning toward the water, she withdraws again, like a sea turtle slipping inside its rock-hard shell.

Thanks for telling me it's not my fault, I seethe. *That was a big help.*

I wait for Kirsten to tell me what's going on, but she doesn't budge. I'm seized with a frightening urge to grab her by the shoulders and shake it out of her, suspending her dangerously over the water if that's what it'll take to get her to talk. But Kirsten has a stronger will than I do. She'd probably let me drop her.

As the picturesque backdrop of Cape May recedes into the background, it suddenly occurs to me that just because Kirsten's miserable doesn't mean I have to be, too. It's a great day, the sun is shining, I'm on the water—all the elements I need to make me content are here. Why should I care if Kirsten is pouting? I don't need her. I can have a good time on my own, can't I?

A brief moment of bravery surfaces, and I turn to Kirsten with my head held high. "When you feel like talking, let me know. I'll be on the other side of the deck," I say, silently congratulating myself as I start heading toward the front of the boat.

Kirsten grabs my arm. "Wait a second—"

I pause, but I still keep my distance.

"Don't go—I'm sorry," she says in a way that makes me want to believe her.

Slowly, I make my way back to the railing. *Hold your ground*, I tell myself. *Don't let her think she can walk all over you.* I don't say anything, waiting for Kirsten to speak first.

"There is something I have to tell you . . . ," she finally says, not looking me in the eye. Her voice is thin, almost hoarse. "I didn't mean to be so distant . . . I've been trying to build up the courage to tell you what's going on . . . but it hasn't been easy."

It hasn't been easy for me, either, I think bitterly to myself.

"I've been talking to my mother a lot," Kirsten begins, swallowing hard. "We've been getting along really well. Better than we have in a long time. Remember when we first came here and you said that maybe my mom had become a different person and I should give her a chance? I think you were right. . . . " Kirsten's voice disappears into the wind.

Staring ahead at the horizon, the water seems as smooth as blue glass. "That's great," I say, though for some reason I don't feel particularly happy for her. "I guess you guys are finally working things out."

Kirsten nods distractedly. "We're trying." A whale-watching boat glides by us on its way out to sea. Kirsten takes a deep breath, then speaks again. "She even offered me a job."

"Your mom?"

Kirsten nods again. "Working with her in the house. Mary's leaving in a month, and Mom will need someone to help her out with things. She thinks I need to settle down and commit myself to something."

I laugh knowingly. "I'm sure you loved hearing that."

She scratches the top of her head. "Actually, I kind of agreed with her."

My pulse quickens. I don't like where this is going. "Wait a minute—I thought you hated it when your mother interfered."

"I don't know . . . what she said this time made sense to me," Kirsten admits. "I feel lost all the time, like I don't belong anywhere or with anyone."

"But you're young," I argue. "You don't have to be tied to anything right now."

"Maybe I *want* to be tied to something for once. Look at you . . . you grew up with the poster family for a perfect home life. Maybe if my life was as predictable as yours, I wouldn't feel so lost."

A flash of anger sparks inside of me. "Am I supposed to take that as a compliment?"

"You know what I mean," she says wearily.

This is so twisted—why on Earth would Kirsten want to be like *me?* "So you want to be more predictable—"

"I want my *life* to be more predictable," Kirsten clarifies. "That's why I've decided to take Mom up on her offer."

I can feel my face crumbling. "What?"

"I'm sorry, Miranda, but I'm not going with you."

My stomach feels like it just took a swan dive down an elevator shaft.

"I can't go," Kirsten repeats again. "Not now."

"What do you mean you can't go?" My throat is closing in on me, the words squeaking out in a tone that's both threatening and pleading. "Of course you can go. . . . "

Kirsten doesn't even have the nerve to look at me. Instead, she stares at the bay unapologetically, as if she's made her decision and it's final. "It's the wrong time for me to be taking off. I need to stick around and spend some time with my mom."

I struggle to fill my lungs with sea air. Thoughts are careening erratically through my brain, colliding with explosive force. Inside, I'm a roiling bundle of emotion churning at twice the speed of sound, while on the outside everything has slowed down to an unbearable eternity. I want to lash out at her, to say something that will pack a punch, catch her off guard, maybe even hurt her. I'm seething.

"You call me up and ask me to go cross-country with you, and now you've just decided on a whim that you don't want to go? I gave up college for this trip, Kirsten!"

Kirsten looks at me for the first time today, her eyes narrow and uncomprehending. "Just because I'm not going doesn't mean you can't travel by yourself."

A blistering wave of heat burns the surface of my skin. In the wake of a luxury yacht that passed before us, the ferry begins rocking unsteadily. "I've never met someone who could ditch people so easily," I answer bitterly.

"I'm not ditching you."

"Then what are you doing?" In the back of my mind, Chloe's prophetic words resurface. She was right about Kirsten after all. "You knew you were going to stay here all along—so why did you bother bringing me here?"

Kirsten's lips tighten. "I didn't plan for it to happen this way. Things happen all the time that you can't predict," she argues. "If *you* were the one who decided not to go on, I would've totally understood."

"That's not the point!" I shout. The family on the bench is staring. "Why make a promise you can't keep?"

"I never *promised* to be your tour guide," Kirsten snaps. "If that's what you thought, then that's *your* problem. We just happened to be two young women who both wanted to travel, so we decided to go together. You knew we were going to split up eventually, didn't you? Or did you think I was going to hold your hand the whole way?"

"I don't know . . . ," I falter, gritting my teeth in humiliation.

"I'm kind of surprised at you, Miranda," Kirsten says in a disapproving voice. "I thought you'd be happy for me. You were so encouraging at first, wanting me to make amends with my mom. Now all you're thinking about is yourself."

Hot tears spring to my eyes, but I fight them back with a fury. There's no way in the world I'm going to let Kirsten see me crying. "I *have* to think of myself," I answer, spitting the words out like venom, "because obviously no one else will."

When we dock at Lewes, Delaware, Kirsten wants to go through with our original plans of spending the day at Cape Henlopen State Park, but I tell her to go ahead without me. In my own small way I want to wreck her plans, just like she wrecked mine. Kirsten doesn't try to change my mind—she just shrugs and goes off in silence. I think she knows there isn't much more to say, at least nothing that we wouldn't regret later.

A few potato chip fragments remain on the bench where the family was sitting, and I flick them off one by one with my fingers, watching them sail violently under the railing and into the waves below.

"I'm so stupid . . ." I slump on the bench, holding my head in my hands. Everyone warned me that I was making a mistake—*everyone*—and I still didn't listen. The only person who supported me was Abigail, but she's only fourteen, what does she know? Even Chloe didn't trust Kirsten and she hardly knew her. It's like there was this giant flashing warning sign that everyone in the world could see except me.

Excuse me for trusting someone. For taking a chance.

I'm not totally blind, though. Thinking back, maybe there were a few red flags I should've paid more attention to. Like, for instance, it *did* seem kind of odd when Kirsten said she wanted to come here to get the car from her mother, considering how they didn't get along in the past. Maybe Kirsten thought I would be a buffer between them and they wouldn't fight so much if I was around. Maybe Kirsten thought if she told her mother we were going to go on this long road trip together, her mother would panic and beg her to stay. Maybe Kirsten never had any intention of going on the trip at all. Maybe since we hardly knew each other she thought she wouldn't have anything to lose.

Maybe, maybe, maybe . . .

I know it's important for Kirsten and her mother to spend time together. And I want them to—just as long as it doesn't get in the way of my plans.

Is that bad?

I compulsively pick at the chipping paint on the underside of the bench with my fingernails. "You know, Kirsten," I mumble into the air, as if my words could be carried by the breeze all the way to Lewes, "the problem with you is that you don't know what you want, and the people around you suffer for it."

"You're not so sure of yourself, either, Miranda," Kirsten would say.

"But at least when I make a decision I stick to it. When I make a promise I try to keep it," I answer, suddenly absorbed in one of those phantom conversations you have long after the argument is over. Why is it that all the best lines dawn on you after the fact? It's so frustrating. "You just do whatever you feel like, regardless of how it's going to affect anyone else."

"I'm surprised, Miranda. I thought you'd be happy for me. But all you're thinking about is yourself."

That one really touched a nerve. What did I say? Something like, "I have to think of myself because no one else will." Scratch that. What I really wanted to say was, "I *am* happy for you, but I don't think you realize how difficult it was for me to give up everything and follow you and then have you bail out on me. I'm not like you, Kirsten. I can't just change my life at the drop of a hat. I don't work that way."

Or maybe something a little more to the point, like, "I hate you, Kirsten. Thanks for ruining my life."

A paint chip drives deep underneath my fingernail, and I let out a little yelp. It doesn't hurt that much, but tears spring to my eyes right away, blurring the sea and sky into one bright watery mass. I squint really hard, wishing I could melt into the landscape and disappear.

I've made up my mind. I'm going home.

The decision was pretty easy, a lot easier than I thought it would be. I want to be gone by the time Kirsten comes back, and since there's really nowhere else for me to go, Connecticut is it. I didn't bother calling my parents. I'll take the bus to New York, then take the train home and call them from the station when I get there. Already my cheeks are burning with humiliation and failure. I've been on my own for about a week now, and the furthest I've gotten is New Jersey. What a loser. Let's just face it— I'm not cut out for adventurous living. I'll probably spend the rest of my life in Connecticut. There's nothing wrong with that, right? I mean, it's probably just meant to be. What's the point of trying to run away from who you really are?

When I get back to the inn I creep up the stairs, hoping not to run into anyone. Thankfully, the house is quiet—no Mrs. Martin or Kyle to get in the way. My clothes are strewn across the bed from this morning, and I quickly shove them into my pack, but I can't zip the zipper. I dump everything out and start over again, carefully rolling them this time, so everything will fit.

"You're back already?" Caroline calls from the doorway, a fresh stack of guest towels in her arms. "You two didn't stay long."

I give her a quick glance, then continue packing. "Kirsten's still there," I say flatly, wondering how much she knows. "I didn't want to stay."

The wooden floors creak as Caroline enters the room. All I see are her brown loafers, the toes touching the bottom of the peach bedskirt. "Did she talk to you?"

I nod. *Khakis, socks, swimsuit . . . I can't forget my swimsuit . . .*

"I'm sure this whole thing is . . . *inconvenient* for you."

"Not at all," I lie, plastering a big, dumb smile on my face. As much as I would love to be straight with Caroline, I don't want her to feel bad. She never promised me anything. "As soon as I'm done packing, I'll be on my way."

"Where are you going?"

Another lie. "I don't know," I say breezily. "I haven't decided yet—Arizona, Alaska, who knows."

Caroline sits down on the bed next to the guidebook my father gave me. "So you're not mad at Kirsten for backing out? She was worried you might not understand."

Somehow, I think Caroline is only saying this

197

to make me feel better. I can't imagine Kirsten giving me much thought at all.

"Of course not." *Big Fat Lie.* "Kirsten has her life, I have mine."

Caroline sighs in a way that tells me she doesn't completely buy my story. "Don't feel like you have to rush off—you know you're welcome to stay here as long as you want. The Gatzkes are arriving this evening, so you and Kirsten can't stay in the guest room, but I have a foldout couch in my bedroom you're welcome to sleep on."

"I appreciate the offer," I answer tiredly, cramming the book into one of the overflowing side pockets, "but you already have a full house to take care of, and I'd just be in the way. I should get moving."

Guilt clouds Caroline's blue eyes. "I feel like we're driving you out."

"Not at all," I say lightly. "You've been more than kind—really."

Caroline shakes her head sadly. "I just don't feel right about this. . . . " She studies me for a moment, then adds, "Look, I know some lovely people nearby who might be able to put you up for a few days—just so you can get your bearings together and figure out what to do next."

"Really . . . it's not necessary."

"You can't just leave, not like this," Caroline says. I start to protest, but Caroline won't hear any of it. "Not another word . . . I insist."

You're going to *love* Daisy and Richard," Caroline says buoyantly as we make the five-minute drive to The Seacrest Inn. "They're special people. I actually stayed here once—during one of my restless episodes—and they seemed so content and happy that it inspired me to get my own place."

I nod absently, wondering if I made a big mistake by not catching the last bus of the day out of town. This whole stupid day has left me feeling wrung out. At this point I'm giving up and just going with the flow. Caroline could drop me off at some dumpy motel on the highway and I wouldn't even care.

The Seacrest Inn, of course, is the furthest thing from a dumpy motel, but it *is* a little bit inland and not on the beach like the name suggests. In the evening light the white mansion almost glows against the sprawling green property. The huge structure is made up of what looks like two identical houses, each about the size of

Caroline's, joined in the middle by a long, rectangular building, forming an "H" shape. Turrets spring up from each corner, like a castle. If I'm lucky, maybe that's where I'll be sleeping tonight.

We park in the circular driveway. A trail of blue forget-me-nots lead us up the path to the front door. "Isn't it gorgeous?" Caroline says.

"Yeah," I answer, stifling a yawn. My eyelids burn, and my head feels like a bowling ball. I hope this doesn't take long—after this day of emotional tug-of-war, all I want to do is crash.

Daisy's waiting for us in the wood-paneled foyer. Caroline greets her with a light peck on the cheek and a brilliant smile. "Where's Richard?" she asks.

"Painting one of the suites in the left wing— what a job that's been!" Daisy turns toward me and extends a pale, slender hand. "It's nice to meet you, Miranda."

At first glance Daisy seems bright and cheerful, her delicate, oval face and rosy lips curved in a permanent smile, but when I look really close I swear I can almost see dark, troubled shadows shifting beneath her fragile skin.

"It's nice to meet you, too," I say, a shiver running up my arm. "Thanks for letting me stay here."

"We're all booked up, unfortunately, but I've set up a cot for you in the stables out back, if that's all right. Don't worry—there aren't any horses in there now." Daisy's voice has this strained lilt to it, making her sound like a cheerful robot.

The stables? I paste a pleasant smile on my face. "Sounds great."

Caroline and I follow Daisy out the French doors to a narrow stone path leading us several yards behind the house. The stables sit low and dark near the edge of the trees, too far from everyone else to be heard if some lunatic came out of the woods and decided to chop me into little bits. Creepy. *I wonder if it's still too late to catch the bus,* I ask myself, gripping the straps of my pack for comfort.

Daisy opens a rickety side door, and the damp smell of stale hay flows over us. Caroline is still smiling brightly, which makes me wonder if she's either lost her mind or at the very least, her sense of smell. Without seeming too obvious, I cover my nose with the back of my hand and step inside the dark stable.

"It's not much, but at least you'll have a place to sleep. . . . " Daisy has disappeared into the black, stinky void, but her eerie voice is close by. Now that no one can see me in the dark, I pinch my nose tightly. I'm busted seconds later when Daisy clicks on a light switch without warning. "And, thankfully, there's electricity—"

Thank goodness for small miracles.

"But no bathroom. You'll have to use the rest room just off the main lobby."

Or the woods . . . where all the lunatics are hiding.

201

Caroline gives me a gentle pat on the shoulder. "So what do you think?"

I glance at the row of stalls made of rotting wood, the rusty horseshoes nailed to the wall, the weblike cracks in the small square window near the door, and my freshly made cot standing proudly in the corner on a mat of old straw.

I clear my throat. "It's perfect!" The instant my eyes get hot and start to blur, I viciously bite the inside of my cheek. *You are not going to feel sorry for yourself, Miranda Burke. No way.*

Daisy fluffs the pillow the same way Caroline does, then puts a chocolate mint on it that has THE SEACREST INN stamped on the gold wrapper. It's so nice, really, the way they're trying to take care of me. "You're welcome to stay as long as you need to," she says sweetly. "And if you need anything, just come to the house. We'll make you breakfast in the morning."

"Thanks so much," I say, feeling a little ashamed at my ingratitude. "You're very kind."

Caroline squeezes my arm. "Here's a little something for you to snack on," she says, handing me a paper bag. "Come over for dinner tomorrow night. Give me a call and we'll pick you up."

"Okay—thanks," I say, biting my lower lip.

"And if you do decide to leave, please don't go without saying good-bye to Kirsten," she says in a motherly voice. "It'll mean a lot to her."

"I won't." I want to kick myself for promising,

because now I'll have to do it. Unless, of course, I *conveniently* forget.

"It's been nice having you." Caroline hugs me with her fleshy arms, my chin pressed awkwardly against the side of her head. "You're a lovely young lady."

Daisy asks me if there's anything else I need, and when I finally convince her that I'm all set, she leaves with Caroline. I watch through the cracked window, their dark forms moving against the fading sunlight as they retreat toward the main house.

It's so quiet. All I hear is the murmur of blood rushing in my ears.

How did I end up here? I ask myself, feeling a tingle of self-pity building in the back of my throat. *I hope you're happy, Kirsten.* A hot mist stings my eyes as I throw one of my T-shirts over the window and wedge a loose board against the door to keep the lunatics out. In one of the stalls I find a rusty pitchfork with a broken wooden handle and I lay it on the floor beside my pack, as an extra line of defense, before settling down to a sorry picnic for one on a cot that smells like horses.

The next morning, in between early morning dreams, I hear a light knock on the stable door. At first I ignore it, my body refusing to move against the thick cocoon of sleep that surrounds me, but eventually the knocking grows so persistent, I open my eyes. Specks of sunlight filter through the T-shirt still hanging over the window.

Then it suddenly dawns on me. *Kirsten.*

I bound out of bed, my foot landing dangerously close to the rusty tines of the pitchfork, and skip across the dirty floor in my bare feet. *I knew she'd change her mind. I knew it. . . .*

"Hi . . . Miranda?"

As soon as I throw open the stable door I'm stunned to see that it's not Kirsten who woke me up but a strange man in his mid-forties with thinning brown hair and a round, fleshy face, holding a breakfast tray. Here I am, in shorts and a tank top, with bed head, and there's a stranger standing at my door. This is not cool.

"Yeah?" I say with just enough attitude to keep

him from getting any bright ideas. I close the door enough so that I'm glaring at him through the crack. "What do you want?"

"I'm Richard," the man says. "Daisy's husband."

"Oh, right," I say, opening the door again. I let out a little nervous laugh, feeling just a tad embarrassed. "Sorry. I didn't realize—"

"I understand," Richard says easily. "You're all by yourself back here. You can never be too careful." He nods to the tray of French toast and juice. "Daisy thought you might like some breakfast. Is there a place where I can set this down?"

"I've got it. Thanks," I say, taking the tray from him. Richard's fingers graze mine as we make the transfer, and I can't help noticing how warm they are compared to Daisy's cold, bony hands. He's also much more animated and buoyant, and his voice is friendly and natural instead of robotic. It's almost like Richard sucked all the life out of his wife and didn't want to give any of it back.

"You got it okay?" he asks.

"Yes, thank you."

I expect Richard to turn around and go back to the main house now that I have my breakfast, but he just stands there looking at me like one of those room service waiters who won't leave until you give them a tip. I'm getting weird vibes from this guy.

Holding the tray under my nose, I take a deep

whiff and close my eyes dreamily. "Ummmm . . . smells delicious. Thanks so much and thank Daisy for me, too," I say with so much drama, you'd think I was one of those movie-of-the-week actresses. "I can't wait to try this French toast. . . ."

But Richard doesn't get the hint. In fact, he hardly budges at all, except to lean with one hand pressed against the side of the building and the other resting on his hip. He looks like he's getting comfortable for the long haul. "So, Daisy tells me you're traveling cross-country."

I freeze in my tracks, the tray balancing precariously on my arm. I don't quite know what to say to him—I mean, I still might do some traveling at some point but I really don't know yet what's going to happen. If I wanted to answer honestly, I could burden Richard with my situation, all the pros and cons, my questions and thoughts, and any other pieces of information about myself that would be pertinent, but the truth is, I really don't want to get into a conversation with this guy.

So in the split second it takes me to formulate an answer, I go with what I'm hoping will lead to the shortest exchange possible. "Yeah . . . "

"That's fantastic," Richard says. "What a wonderful opportunity."

I back away from him a little. "It should be fun."

"You know I did the same thing when I was your age?"

Thanks for sharing . . . can I eat my breakfast now?

I smile politely. "Really?"

Richard puckers his lips wistfully and hooks his fingers in the belt loops of his pants. He looks extremely pleased with himself. "That was about twenty years ago, if you can believe it."

I sure can.

"I spent a year roaming," Richard continues. "Just me and my backpack bumming around, trying to find work whenever I could. It was great. There were days that would go by when I had no money in my pockets and I wondered where my next meal was coming from. I tell you, there's nothing like an empty stomach to give you a little perspective on what's important in life."

Richard drones on and on, hardly ever stopping to take a breath. I stare off into space, back up a little, and even start to close the door, but the man is totally oblivious to all the clues I'm giving him. He even pushes the door open again to tell me about how he worked in a tuna-packing plant in Alaska. It's obvious he couldn't care less whether or not I'm actually listening to him—he just likes the sound of his own voice.

When Richard finally stops to take a breath, I pounce. "It sounds like you had a fantastic time. Thanks for telling me about it and for bringing breakfast. I hope you don't mind, but I'm kind of hungry. . . . "

"Go right ahead, I don't mind at all," he says, and just stands there, like I'm supposed to eat in front of him.

Go away . . . go away . . . go away . . . Maybe if I think hard enough, he'll pick up my psychic vibrations.

Richard continues on, still oblivious. "So who are you going with?" he asks.

Going with? Is this a dating question? I miserably sip my orange juice. "Excuse me?"

"On your trip—who are you going with?"

"Oh . . . uh, no one, I guess. It's just me—alone," I mumble, imagining myself somewhere more pleasant. The dentist's chair is the first place that springs to mind.

Richard shakes his head and clucks his tongue like a chicken. "In my day, traveling by yourself was a fairly safe thing to do—I used to even go hitchhiking, if you can believe it, and get rides from truckers. But it's not something I'd recommend nowadays. Especially for an extremely attractive young woman like yourself. . . ."

Here we go . . . a hot, embarrassed smile distorts my lips. There's something in Richard's dark eyes that makes me want to crawl out of my skin. Maybe it's the fact that he's talking to my chest.

"Some weird individuals like to prey on beautiful young women. They get sick ideas," he says, not looking too stable himself.

Actually, I think I'm *going to be sick.*

"You know, I'm not feeling too great this morning," I suddenly say, moving away. "Thanks for everything."

And before Richard has a chance to say anything else, I slam the door in his face.

My appetite is totally shot, thanks to Richard and my nervous stomach. I sit on the cot and wait for a long time until I'm sure he's not peeking at me through a crack in the stable boards, and then change into my jeans and a baggy T-shirt. I drink the rest of the orange juice but fling the syrupy slices of French toast like Frisbees into the woods and watch while two squirrels and a baby chipmunk battle it out for the prize. The squirrels dominate the scene, eventually pushing out the little one completely. I wait until the squirrels are busy gorging themselves, then I take the last slice and toss it to the baby chipmunk so he'll have a whole piece to himself.

Gathering up my stuff, I head to the house to wash up. Daisy's on the back patio chatting with a few guests as I skip up the back stairs. Even in the bright light of morning, her skin still has an eerie, translucent glow.

"How are you this morning?" she asks.

"Fine, thanks."

"Would you like some breakfast? We have some lovely banana nut muffins this morning."

Hold on a second. I thought Daisy had sent me the French toast . . . at least that's what Richard said. . . . It doesn't take a nuclear physicist to piece this one together—Richard is a lech of the highest order. I'm starting to understand where that tired, traumatic look lurking behind Daisy's eyes is coming from.

I give Daisy a sympathetic smile. "It sounds great, but I'm not really hungry this morning. I think I'm just going to wash up and then head to the beach."

Quickly, I walk through the foyer to the bathroom near the main desk, hoping to avoid running into Richard again, and lock the door behind me. I run the faucet full blast and let the water flow over my arms. Cupping my hands under the cool stream, I splash my face, allowing a few drops of water to drip down my hairline, then I comb the curls back with my fingers into a ponytail. In the greenish-yellow light of the bathroom my own face looks strange to me—like I'm looking at someone else.

"Miranda Burke," I murmur, studying the odd landscape of my mouth, nose, and chin. I see myself and I hear my name, but somehow the pieces don't fit together right.

Who am I?

I try on different labels to find a correct match. "Miranda Burke, world traveler."

Nah. It's too ridiculous.

"Miranda Burke, Yale student."

Too stuffy.

"Miranda Burke, loving daughter and loyal friend."

Please.

"Miranda Burke, person with great potential who chickened out."

That sounds about right.

I squirt a gob of toothpaste on my toothbrush. I'm still pretty mad at Kirsten for what happened yesterday, but I'm more sad and disappointed than anything else. My heart aches for all the experiences I'm going to miss out on. We would've had a pretty great time on the road together, and Kirsten was just the person to give me the nudge I needed—always daring, full of energy, ready to take on whatever came her way. It was my fault for depending so much on her, but I would've never had the courage to do it on my own.

So instead of immersing myself in new territories and adventures, I'll be involved in class schedules and dorm rooms. That's not so bad. I'm simply exchanging one set of experiences for another. And my parents will be so happy—I won't have to feel guilty about leaving them behind. Dad even owes me a car for not going on the trip. With so much to gain, though, why does it feel like I'm losing out big time?

I spit in the sink and rinse my mouth. *That*

settles it, then—I guess I'm going home, I tell myself, licking the chalky outline of toothpaste still remaining on my upper lip. *It's for the best . . . really. A year from now you'll be thanking Kirsten for ditching you.*

"Excuse me, do you have a phone I can use?" I ask Gina, the young woman behind the front desk.

Gina fiddles with the end of her long braid and smiles. "Are you the world traveler Richard and Daisy have been talking about?"

My chest caves in. "Yes—I mean no," I stutter. "I mean I haven't exactly gone anywhere, yet."

"That's so exciting!" Gina squeals spastically. "You're so lucky! I've never been anywhere. I was born in Cape May and I've lived here my whole life."

"Really?" I don't know why, but for some reason this really shocks me. It's not like I've been so far myself. "I'm sure you'll have a chance one of these days to visit some interesting, faraway place."

"I don't know," Gina says wistfully, twirling her braid around a pen. "People like you are meant to travel to exciting places. Not me—I'm meant to stay put."

"That's not true," I argue. "You can do anything you want. If you want to travel, you should do it."

Gina pouts her lips, apparently unconvinced. "I don't know . . . ," she answers, wrinkling her nose.

213

"Oh, you wanted to use the phone? You can use the one in the office." She points to a door behind her. "You probably have to check up on your next destination, right?"

"Yeah," I answer, letting the air ease out of my lungs. "That's exactly what I'm doing."

Mom, it's me, Miranda."

"Sweetheart! How are you?" There's a muffled sound at the other end, then I hear Mom calling to Dad, who's probably in the den with his nose in the *Wall Street Journal*. "Sorry we didn't get your call the other night—we got home late. I thought you'd call back the next night, but we didn't hear from you."

"I had a lot of things going on," I explain.

There's a popping sound as my dad picks up the extension. "Hello?"

"Hi, Dad . . . how's it going?" I lean back in the office chair and swivel from side to side.

"Where are you, Pumpkin?" he asks.

"I'm still in Cape May." I can hear the clicking of plates and glasses in the background. It's a homey, comforting sound. "Are you guys just finishing up with breakfast?"

"I'm doing the dishes," Mom says. "I want to get out to garden early—it's supposed to be a hot one today."

I close my eyes and pretend for a moment that I'm there, drowsily reading the morning paper over a plate of Mom's famously yummy pancakes.

"Did Abby get my postcard?" I ask.

"Yesterday. She was thrilled," Mom says.

"I'm glad."

Dad clears his throat. "Why are you still in Cape May?"

My stomach hardens like a rock. "Kirsten's Mom needed some help at the inn," I explain. "Besides, we're not in a big rush."

Okay, what was that all about? Did you suddenly develop an allergy to telling the truth?

"Are you girls having a good time?" Mom asks.

"Kirsten—" My tongue suddenly freezes. When I try to speak again, my mouth feels like it's taken on a life of its own. "Yeah, we're having a great time."

Liar.

"We really enjoyed meeting her," Mom continues on over the hiss of the faucet. "She seems like a very nice girl."

"She's great," I say. "We get along well."

What's wrong with you? shouts a voice inside my head. *Tell them what happened. Tell them Kirsten ditched you. Tell them you want to come home. . . .*

"Miranda, are you still there?" Mom asks.

"Uh, yeah . . . "

"Is something wrong?" Mom picks up on this

stuff right away. Not only does she seem to possess psychic powers, but I swear she's got a lie detector built into her brain. "You sound funny—something must be bothering you."

Here's your chance. She's giving you the opening. . . .

I take in a deep breath. "Nothing's wrong."

Mom still seems skeptical. "So you're not calling us because you're in trouble?"

"No!" I'm sorry, but I'm slightly offended by that comment—even if there's a touch of truth to it.

"I thought for sure you were calling because you ran out of money already," Dad jokes.

"I have plenty of money," I answer. *So there.* "I just thought it would be nice to check in and see how everyone's doing."

"That's so *sweet.*" Mom's starting in already; I can hear her voice getting thicker and more emotional every second. "We miss you."

In the center of my chest I feel a dark, empty hole opening up, like something's missing inside of me. For just five minutes I wish I was a little kid again and could curl up on my parents' laps, telling them every thought that popped into my head. The world was safe and perfect, and I didn't even know it at the time. There weren't any secrets. Now, things have changed. I can't tell them everything that's happening in my life, not if I want to learn to handle things on my own. In one way it makes me feel strong, but mostly, it just makes me sad.

"I miss you guys, too," I answer, blinking back tears. I wonder if they know how much. "Look, I've got to get going," I say, clearing my throat. "I have a lot to do today."

"We don't want to keep you," Mom says.

Tell them the plans fell through and you're coming home. . . . What are you waiting for?

"Call us in a few days," Dad says. "Be good."

"I will . . . " The receiver feels slippery in my sweaty hand. I want so badly to tell them I'm coming home, but I can't. I don't feel any rational control over what I'm doing—I'm operating solely on instincts. "I love you guys."

"We love you," they say together. "Call us soon."

And before I have the chance to say anything else, I hang up.

Have you totally lost your mind?

I lean my head against the back of the chair, trying to make sense of why I just sabotaged my own plan to go home. Maybe it was simply that I was too proud to admit defeat. But there was something more to it—something I can't quite name. And it's scaring me.

"Miranda?"

The throaty rasp of Richard's voice yanks me out of my thoughts. I dry my eyes with the back of my hand and whirl around in the chair to see his round body blocking the darkened doorway of the office.

"Ah, sorry," I apologize, sitting up straight in the chair. "Gina told me I could use the phone in here—"

"That's all right," Richard interrupts. His eyes bear down on me in a way that makes me want to cover up with a blanket. "I was walking by and saw the light—I thought someone left it on."

Likely story. I fold my arms in front of my chest. "Nope, it's just me."

Now please leave . . . you're creeping me out.

"Are you making plans for your next stop?" Richard asks, moving closer. He walks around to my side of the desk and leans against it, his legs only inches away from mine, then runs a hand through his thinning hair.

"Sort of," I murmur. *Can he tell I've been crying? My face must be all red and blotchy. I really, really, really want to leave, but I don't want him to get a sick thrill from freaking me out.*

Richard gives me a nauseating smile. "Where's it going to be?"

My heart is thumping loudly against my rib cage. "I don't know yet."

"I can help you if you need ideas," Richard says. His voice is so smooth and friendly that it makes me second-guess myself all the time. One minute he's seems like a nice enough guy and I'm sure I've got it all wrong, but then the next minute he looks at me a certain way and something in my gut tells me it's not right. It's not right at all.

"I have plenty of ideas of my own, thank you," I answer, slowly rolling the chair away from him. I could make a run for the door, but I don't want to be obvious.

"You look like the romantic type," Richard whispers, staring deep into my eyes. "You should go somewhere romantic like an island off the coast of Maine or a little cabin in the mountains. I've always wanted to do that. Wouldn't it be fun?"

"Richard—"

Looking up at the doorway, I see Daisy's ghostly figure standing there, her big, dark eyes glaring ominously at the two of us. I freeze. The gracious smile has evaporated, replaced with a look of disgust but definitely not surprise. I get the feeling Richard does this sort of thing all the time.

Creep.

"Yes, dear?" Richard hops away from me and practically runs to his wife. "I was just having a chat with Miranda. What do you need?"

Daisy flinches when he tries to touch her. "I need to speak to you in private, *please.*"

Richard follows her out of the office. "I'll be right back, Miranda," he says, pointing at me. "Don't go anywhere."

Fat chance, sleazeball. While Richard is trying to convince his wife he's really not a scumbucket, I sneak out the door.

As soon as I open the stable door and take a whiff of that awful smell of hay, I really start bawling. I don't know what's triggered this outburst, but I think Richard put me over the edge. I throw myself on the cot, burying my soggy face in the pillow, and let it rip. My cries reverberate in the dank horse stalls until every last bit of air is squeezed out of my lungs. Then, I take in a huge sobbing breath and start all over again.

It doesn't take long at all for the self-pity to kick in. *My life is totally falling apart. I don't have anywhere to go. I don't have any friends. No one cares about me. I don't know what I'm doing with my life . . .* you know, the usual melodramatic stuff. The tantrum comes to an abrupt halt at the recent memory of Richard leering at me in the office, telling me to wait for him. Would he come looking for me? I don't plan on sticking around to find out.

With eyes that are practically swollen shut, I shove my nightclothes into my bag, gather up the trash from last evening's picnic, and scrawl a hasty note to Daisy to thank her for letting me stay in the stable. As the tip of the pen scratches across a torn-out page of my travel journal, I can't help but think what a strange, unexpected turn my life has taken. The world seems turned upside down, and what's so terrifying is I don't know how to make it right again. With nothing to cling to, I'm scared I'm going to fall right off the edge.

Through the cracked window I catch a glimpse of Richard's balding head as he paces the foyer, staring out at the stables, while Daisy waters the flower beds on the back walkway, keeping watch over her snake of a husband. By now Richard knows I didn't wait for him in the office, and my guess is, he's planning on looking for me here as soon as Daisy's out of sight, which thankfully doesn't seem to be anytime soon. I leave the note on the cot and, heaving the pack on my shoulders, walk outside, heading straight for the road. Richard stares at me as I walk across the lawn, not daring to make a move under the watchful eye of his wife. I resist the urge to give him a taunting little wave at the road's edge.

What now? Getting out of town is definitely a priority—maybe I'll hike to The Wildwoods, the beach resorts nearby. Even though Kirsten swindled me out of two hundred bucks for a car I'm never going to drive, I still have a bunch of travel money left I could use to maybe rent a room for a couple of days. You know, lay on the beach a little, let the water clear the last few days out of my head. It sounds like a lovely idea, but I know I don't have the guts to be by myself even for such a short time. Whenever the next bus leaves for New York, I have a feeling I'll be on it.

The road feels solid beneath my feet, and the warm wind dries my tears. With the pack on my back, I feel like I'm actually going somewhere, a self-contained unit built for travel. For a moment I pretend I'm not in New Jersey but on the Pacific Coast, walking south through California, not knowing anyone for thousands of miles and having to rely upon myself for survival. Just the idea of it sends a panicky thrill shooting up my spine and radiating through my limbs.

You could do it, you know, if you had to, a voice whispers in my head. *You're a smart person. You could take care of yourself.*

I march forward, the gravel crunching underfoot with each step.

A car horn honks, and I turn around to see a little blue Ford Escort trailing behind me. *Oh, God . . . it's Kirsten.* I wanted so badly to just slip out of town, unnoticed, never even bothering to say good-bye. There's something dignified about being mysterious. It figures she'd have to mess that up for me, too.

Kirsten rolls down the window and sticks her arm out, waving at me. "What are you doing?"

"Walking," I answer curtly.

"Where to? I'll give you a ride."

I hesitate for a minute. It's weird seeing her. "No thanks."

"Come on," Kirsten says, goading me. "You own half the car, you should at least try it out."

What's going on here? I wonder. *Is she going to tell me she's changed her mind about staying? Does she want to take the trip after all?*

Kirsten leans over and opens the passenger side door. I don't know why, but I suddenly find myself throwing my pack in the back and sliding into the front seat. The sticky vinyl upholstery smells like suntan lotion, and the dashboard is covered with old stickers of flowers and spaceships. I wait for Kirsten to talk first.

"So how are things at The Seacrest?" Kirsten asks, putting her foot to the floor. "Mom says they've got you in the stables."

I debate whether or not to tell her about the hay smell and creepy Richard, but the last thing I want is for Kirsten to feel sorry for me. I want her to believe I'm better off without her—even though it might not be true.

"Things are great," I say easily. I roll down the window and rest my arm on the door frame. "It's comfortable and quiet."

"So slimy Richard didn't try to paw you? You lucked out," Kirsten says with a wry laugh. "I don't know *what* my mother sees in that freaky couple."

Kirsten turns the radio to a rock station and drums her fingers against the steering wheel in time to the beat. "Where are you headed?"

I stare out at the sparkling beach as it rushes past us. "What do you care?"

"Jeesh, you don't have to be so defensive. I was just asking a question."

I still can't tell if Kirsten's changed her mind or not. It'd be just like her to make me sweat, waiting until the last possible second to tell me.

Kirsten yawns loudly. "I came looking for you, Miranda, because I wanted to tell you how sorry I am about yesterday. I spent the whole day walking around, thinking about things. I know I didn't handle the situation very well. . . . "

"You're right about that," I answer flatly.

"And I can understand why you would be angry with me."

"I'm glad."

Neither of us say anything for a long while. The elaborate arguments that played out so carefully in my head fall away, and I can't remember any of the brilliant remarks I wanted to fling at her. Now there's nothing to say.

"I don't want you to be mad," Kirsten says finally, pursing her thin lips.

My toes tap an unsteady rhythm against the dirty floor mat. "Sorry to disappoint you."

"I really gave this a lot of thought yesterday," Kirsten explains, turning down the radio. "What it boils down to is this—I'm terrified of making the same mistakes my mother did. And to be honest, if things continue the way they've been going, I'm heading straight for disaster. But now I have the opportunity to do something about it, and I'm going to take that chance. You can understand that, can't you?"

I can feel the muscles in my jaw hardening. "Well, yeah—but I don't understand why you have to do it now. Why can't we just continue on as planned and then you can settle down like you want? What difference would a year make?"

"I'm just following my gut on this one," she says. "Like I said before, this is something I've got to do for myself. I'm just sorry it's messing things up for you."

"Me, too."

Well, there's my answer. I guess she didn't change her mind after all. In the seconds it takes for this realization to sink in, I grip the edge of the seat, bracing myself for the final, crushing blow of disappointment. To my surprise, it never comes. Instead, there's this gentle wave washing over me, as warm as sunlight, telling me everything's going to be okay. I don't need Kirsten. Things will turn out just fine without her.

"Which way are you headed?" she asks. "I can take you anywhere you need to go."

There's no point in dragging this out. It only makes it harder. "Right here is fine."

"Here?" Kirsten asks incredulously, looking at the empty residential street to our right and the tiny post office and diner straight ahead. She pulls over to the side. "There's nothing here."

I reach behind the seat and grab my pack. "I hope this really turns things around for you," I say. "Good luck."

Kirsten stares at me through thick black eyelashes, her eyes almost tinged with regret. "Yeah— I think things are going to get better," she says. I open the door, but she holds me back. "Before you go . . . reach under the glove compartment. There's something under the seat I want to give you."

I look at her, then lean over and run my fingers under the seat. I pull out Kirsten's road atlas with a white envelope sticking out of it.

"That's the money you gave me for the car," Kirsten says, touching the envelope.

I'm so relieved. I thought I'd never see that money again. "Thanks."

"And the atlas is yours, too. You'll need it more than I will," she adds. "Go ahead, open it up."

"Where?"

"Anywhere."

Slowly, I thumb through the pages. The maps are covered with yellow sticky notes, and each one has Kirsten's scrawl on it. "What's this all about?" I ask.

"Mom and I wrote down the names, addresses, and phone numbers of everyone we knew across the country so if you're ever in trouble you'll have someone to get in touch with. We also wrote down some things we remembered about each of the different places, you know, like a guidebook. If you really want to travel, Miranda, you should still do it. Don't change your life because of me."

Gently, I close the atlas. Through all the murky emotions and confusion I've been feeling over the last twenty-four hours, Kirsten's words cut through it all, resonating in my ears like a crystal bell: *Don't change your life because of me. . . .*

That's exactly what I did.

offee?" a waitress with pink-framed glasses and white sneakers asks, putting a mug on the counter in front of me.

"Sure," I answer, trying to lean my bulky pack against the stool without it toppling over.

"Cream? Sugar?" She slaps a laminated menu down that says TEDDY'S DINER.

"Uh, both—I guess." I'm not really here to eat, even though I did feed Richard's breakfast to the squirrels. After Kirsten dropped me off, I suddenly remembered something I forgot to do. "Do you have a pay phone I can use?"

"Out back near the bathroom," the waitress says. "Hey, are you going to order anything?"

"Scrambled eggs and toast," I say, glancing at the first thing I see on the menu.

I slide off the stool and squeeze past a table or two to the back room, which is a dark, narrow hallway crowded with cardboard boxes of napkins and straws. The heavy smell of chlorine trickles through the bathroom door. I find my dad's calling card and punch the number into the key-pad.

"Hi, Jayson, it's Miranda."

"Hey, M! How's my little sister?" he asks. "I haven't heard from you in a while."

Instead of tiptoeing around the subject, I just lay it all out for him. "Kirsten bailed on me. We're not going on the trip."

"Oh, man—I'm really sorry to hear that," he says.

"Sure you are," I say sarcastically.

"No, really. I know you were really looking forward to this trip. Disappointed?"

"Slightly."

"Are you home now?"

Through the doorway I can see the waitress putting a plate of scrambled eggs on the counter near my stool. "I'm in a diner in Jersey, trying to decide what to do next."

"Do Mom and Dad know?" my brother asks.

"Not yet," I answer. "I know I should go home, but it just feels too soon. I don't know what to do. Any ideas?"

The other end of the line is quiet for a minute. I can almost hear Jay scratching the back of his head and wrinkling his nose up the way he always does when he's lost in thought. "You could come here and stay for a little while—at least until you figure out what you want to do."

"Virginia?" I lean against a carton of paper

231

towels. Why didn't I think of it before? "Are you going to be okay with that?"

"Sure—why not?" he says. We can work something out."

I wish my brother was here in person so I could give him a great big hug. "Jay, this is so great! Thank you so much!"

"If I leave within the hour I should be able to get up there by sometime this evening."

"Don't bother, Jay," I protest. "I'll find a way to get there on my own."

"How do you plan on doing that?"

I kick the side of the carton with the toe of my hiking boot. "I'll take a bus or something, I don't know."

"No way—I'm coming to get you." Jayson's voice has suddenly taken on this commanding tone that makes him sound just like Dad. *Now that's scary.* I have to admit, it would be easy to get a ride from Jayson—I wouldn't have to worry about a thing. But part of me wants to take a chance and see what happens.

"Forget it," I answer. "I'll figure it out and give you a call when I get close to Charlottesville."

"Are you sure?"

"I'm sure. I'll be fine—really," I answer. "I'm looking forward to it."

Jay snickers. "Mom and Dad would have a fit if they knew."

"I know," I say with a laugh. "Isn't it great?"

The man sitting next to me at the counter has a red baseball cap and a chalky-white outline around his lips from the powdered doughnut he's eating. He eats slowly and methodically, taking one sip of coffee from a thick white mug for every two bites of doughnut.

I've never eaten by myself in restaurant before and I have to say it's a little strange. When you have someone sitting across from you, there's a point of reference, something to concentrate on, a crutch to keep you from feeling self-conscious. But when no one's there, what do you do? I could stare like a zombie at my eggs or the napkin dispenser or the hairy arms of the cook at the grill. Or I could be friendly and try to strike up a conversation with Doughnut Man. I wouldn't know where to begin with that one.

"Excuse me," I say shyly, reaching in front of him to snag a bottle of ketchup. I try to shut myself off from what's going on around me, the way I saw people in New York do, pretending I'm in my very own private box with thick Plexiglas walls. I have more important things to worry about than eating by myself. Like how to get to Virginia.

"You'd better take it easy on that stuff," Doughnut Man says dryly, watching me dump a pile of ketchup on my eggs. "It'll rot your gut."

"More than doughnuts will?" I tease back.

Where did that come from? For a second there I totally forgot myself. It's like someone else took over.

Doughnut Man adjusts the visor on his baseball cap. "Doughnuts are good for you," he says, pounding his chest. "They make your heart strong. Just ask Gary over there."

"Ask me what?" Gary is sitting at the other end of the counter, shirtsleeves rolled up to his elbows, working on a doughnut of his own.

"Doughnuts are good for you, right?"

Gary nods without missing a beat. "I have two every morning—doctor's orders."

I laugh. "Well, *my* doctor recommends ketchup."

Doughnut Man shakes his head. "I think you'd better get a second opinion," he answers, taking a sip of coffee. "So where you headed?"

"Excuse me?" I heard what he said, but I'm not sure if I should answer. Richard's got me all freaked out about talking to people. I mean, you're not supposed to tell strangers about

234

yourself, right? Especially when you're all alone?

"I noticed your pack," Doughnut Man says. "You going camping?"

"I'm going to visit my brother," I answer, scooping up a bit of egg with my toast. Something deep inside me says, *It's all right, you can talk to this guy.* I don't know if I can trust the voice inside me, but I do know that this is a crowded, public place, there's a pay phone only a few steps away, and I don't have a clue how to get to Virginia. Maybe this guy can help.

Doughnut Man brushes his powdery fingers on his blue jeans. "Does he live here in town?"

"No, he's outside Charlottesville, Virginia," I answer.

"Is that so? My wife is from Virginia—Manassas. It's a suburb of D.C. Charlottesville is a bit farther down."

I can't believe my luck. "So you've been there?"

"Lots of times." Doughnut Man doesn't look at me when he talks, but stares straight ahead where the cook is standing at the grill. I don't mind it at all. "Got to visit the in-laws, you know."

I take a long drink of my coffee. "What's the best way to get there?"

"Well, the most direct route is to take the ferry to Lewes, then catch Route 1, but I like to go—"

I cut him off. "I don't have a car. . . . "

"Right. Let me see . . . " Doughnut Man scratches his chin, leaving a fine dust of powder in his whiskers. "There's a bus station at Lewes, I think. You should be able to catch something from there."

"If I were you, I'd call first," the waitress with the pink glasses says, refilling Doughnut Man's mug. "They might have only one or two buses per day."

Good point. I go back to the pay phone and flip through the Yellow Pages. I find a number for Carolina Trailways.

"There's a bus for D.C. that's leaving in two hours," I tell them when I get back to the counter. "They say I should be able to get a connecting bus there."

"You'd better get a move on," the waitress says. "It's going to take you over an hour to take the ferry across."

"Right," I say, gulping down the last of my coffee. There's a fuzzy tingling sensation right below my rib cage. Things are starting to happen.

"You know you're going to need a reservation, don't you?" Doughnut Man says.

"A reservation? For what?"

"The ferry," the waitress says. "Especially with tourist season, there's no way you can get on there without a reservation."

A burst of heat breaks over my forehead. There's only one bus leaving Lewes today for D.C., and if I'm not on it, I'm going to have to spend another night here—who knows where. *I don't remember making a reservation with Kirsten,*

I think, but my memory is cloudy. Maybe Caroline took care of it for us the night before.

"I don't have one," I stammer numbly. "I didn't know."

The waitress rests her chapped, overworked hands on the counter. "I'll tell you what. I know someone who works over there at the terminal, I'll put in a call for you. What's your name?"

"Miranda Burke," I say, taking one last bite of toast. "Thanks so much for doing this, I really appreciate it."

The waitress gives me a reserved smile. "No problem."

"Do you want a ride to the ferry?" Doughnut Man asks. "It's only a mile or so away, but you'll get there a lot quicker."

I wrestle with the straps to get the backpack on. My muscles strain under the weight. "No thanks," I say firmly. My heartbeat is picking up speed already. I'm about to head for the door when I remember my bill. "Oh, how much do I owe you?" I say to the waitress.

"Three-fifty," she answers.

I shove my hands in my pockets. Empty. I groan inwardly, remembering that my money is tucked away *somewhere* in my pack. Shaking off the pack, I rest it on my stool and fumble through one pocket to the next to find some cash.

"Don't worry about it," Doughnut Man says, watching me. "I got you covered."

"Thank you, but I've got money," I say breathlessly.

"Forget about it. Go catch your boat," he says in a way that I can't refuse.

"All right," I say with a grateful smile, zipping up my pack. "You're very kind. Oh, one last thing—which way do I go?"

Doughnut Man puckers his powdery lips. "Take a left out the door, then take another left at the next intersection. You should see it from there."

If running a mile doesn't sound like much to you, try doing it with fifty million pounds strapped to your back. I feel like I'm in training for the Olympics. I've never been much of an athlete and in gym class when Mr. Grant made us run track, Chloe and I used to walk it whenever his back was turned. We used to think he was mean, but now I think that maybe he was doing us a favor. If Mr. Grant was here now I'd gladly run ten miles for him, as long as I could take off this dumb pack.

By the time I make it to the terminal, I'm sweating like a pig. They're already boarding. I run up to the reservations desk panting, my hair frizzed out in all directions.

"Miranda Burke," I wheeze to the lady behind the counter.

"You have a reservation?" she asks.

I nod. The woman checks the computer. It seems to be taking a while, and as I'm starting to catch my breath I get this terrible feeling that maybe the waitress was too busy and forgot to call or that she lied about it altogether and everyone in the diner had a good laugh at my expense.

"Here it is—" the woman finally says, much to my relief. "And it looks like it's been all taken care of."

"Excuse me?"

"Your ticket has been paid," she says.

I wipe a drop of sweat off my brow. "You're kidding."

The woman hands me a ticket. "You'd better hurry, the ferry's about to leave."

I sprint through the terminal to the dock and make it through just as the gate is about to close. I climb up the stairs to the top level, walking past the spot where Kirsten gave me the terrible news that doesn't seem so terrible anymore, and make my way to the front of the boat so I can see where I'm going.

This is the one," says the woman in her thirties standing next to me as we watch the red-striped Carolina Trailways bus take a wide turn into the parking lot of Ace Hardware.

When the bus driver opens the doors, I move all the way to the back of the empty bus and unload my pack, shoving it into the overhead rack, then sink my weary muscles into a plush seat. In three and a half hours I'll be in Washington, D.C., and then I'll switch buses and continue on for about the same amount of time to Charlottesville, where I'll meet up with my brother. So in just the past few days I'll have gone from Connecticut to Virginia, and half of the distance I'll have done on my own. Each mile farther away from Connecticut is a notch on my belt of experience.

But who's counting?

I don't know how things will work out when I get there. Jayson and I might get sick of each other after a couple of days, and I might just give up and go back home. Or maybe I won't want to go home at all but will continue on by myself, to finish the plans I'd made with Kirsten. Who knows? Maybe Kirsten actually did me a big favor. At least that's what I'll keep telling myself.

As the bus pulls out of the parking lot and starts rolling down Route 1, the little town of Lewes fades behind me like memory. I close my eyes and never look back. Not even once.

Here's a look at the next book in the

series.

EXIT #2: BUYING TIME

Sitting on the wooden bench directly across from me at the Charlottesville bus station are two teenagers with their arms wrapped around each other like they have only one minute left to live. It's sweet—in a really pathetic sort of way. Loverboy is slumped over his girlfriend, practically smothering her with the hollow of his neck. It's a wonder she can get any air in there. They both have their eyes closed (which is why I haven't been busted for staring), and their lips are all pouty and sad. My guess is they're going their separate ways for the summer. I'm sure it feels like the end of the world to them now, but give it a few weeks. Before you know it, he's going to be smothering some other girl and she's going to be having a summer fling with the beach boy of her dreams. By the time fall rolls around, they won't even remember each other's names.

Hey, I'm not saying true love doesn't happen. I'm just saying it doesn't happen as often as most people want to believe. *Like* and *love* are confused all the time. And, frankly, it's a bit insulting to those of who are holding out for the real thing.

"Hey, M, sorry to keep you waiting. . . ."

I peel my eyes away from the Comatose Love Twins to see Jayson's tall, muscular frame standing over me. He runs his hand through his thick reddish-brown hair, which leaves a few tufts sticking up, and smiles at me with his gold-green eyes. Behind him, I watch two grown women nearly collide as one fixates on his broad shoulders and the other one ogles his blue jeans. As always, Jayson is completely oblivious.

Before you get any weird ideas, let me explain that Jay's my *brother*, and, *no, he's not available*, thank you very much. He's totally in love with his gorgeous, smart, funny (did I mention rich?) girl-friend, Valerie, and believe me, it's for real. In fact, they're probably going to get married. And I'm going to be a bridesmaid. So, for now, you're just going to have to drool.

Jayson twirls the car keys with his fingers. "I couldn't find a parking space. Hope you weren't waiting long."

"It's okay—I had some entertainment," I say wryly, handing him my ten-ton backpack. We hug briefly. Hugging is still a new thing for us—something we started when Jay went away to college last year. I kind of like it. It's a lot better than when we used to wrestle in the den and he'd sit on me, squeezing all the air out of my lungs until I was on the verge of passing out.

A crackly voice comes over the P.A. system to announce a departing bus. Jay presses his lips together and smiles. He looks so much like Mom when he does that. "So how was the trip?"

I could tell him about the charley horse I got in my leg from sitting too long, or the screaming baby across the aisle from me, or even about the mysterious smell of vomit no one could seem to locate—but I don't want Jay to call me a whiner. He's already mistakenly under the impression that since I'm the firstborn girl, I'm a spoiled princess.

"It was great . . . went by just like *that*," I say, snapping my fingers. My fingers, along with the rest of my body, feel coated in a sticky layer of bus slime that I'm praying will melt with a little soap and a strong stream of hot water. "I slept almost the whole way."

Jay flashes me a doubtful smirk. "Val's anxious to see you. I told her we'd meet her for dinner if you're up for it."

"Cool. How are things going with you guys?"

"Fine," Jay answers as we head toward the exit, lumbering under the weight of my pack. "Man, what do you have in here?"

"Stuff," I say. With cramped legs, I struggle to follow alongside my brother. "Can we get burgers tonight? I'm kind of in the mood for a big fat cheeseburger and a side of onion rings."

As Jay opens the door for me, hot Virginia air blasts into the chilled bus station. "Whatever you want, M."

Before we leave, I take one last look over my shoulder at the couple on the bench. Someone should give them a poke to make sure they're still alive. They haven't even moved an inch.

I'm sorry, but that's just not natural.

Heading westbound on I-64, Jay's black Saturn makes the steady climb up Afton Mountain toward Waynesboro. Rocky cliffs rise up to the right of the highway as we near the southernmost tip of Shenandoah National Park. Jay tells me there's a scenic highway nearby called Skyline Drive that follows the crests of the Blue Ridge Mountains for a hundred miles or so. The terrain is so green and beautiful—an endless, graceful chain of gently rolling peaks—so different from the little tree-lined streets of Greenwich, our hometown back in Connecticut. I'm not sure what I was expecting this area to look like, but I never dreamed it would be this stunning. I beg Jay to take a detour up Skyline Drive, but he says it's too late in the day. We'll have to do it some other time.

For now, I have to settle for I-64.

"So Kirsten ditched you?" Jay asks.

I push the seat back to stretch my legs. "She didn't *ditch* me," I answer more sharply than I mean to. The wound is still a little raw, I guess. "She just decided to stay with her mother for a while. They're working some things out."

"That's right—they never did get along too well." He bites his lower lip thoughtfully and thumps his fingers on the steering wheel in time to a song on the radio.

I twirl my long curly hair into a loose knot to get it off the back of my sticky neck. "I mean, I'm glad they're working on their relationship and everything, but why do they have to do it *now?* Can't they wait until after the trip? Am I being totally selfish?"

He raises his thick eyebrows and exhales. "A little, but it's completely understandable, given the situation."

Jay's approval spurs me on. "After all, *she* was the one who asked *me* to go across the country with *her. . . .*" I rant, my blood pressure shooting up ten points. It's hard to think about everything Kirsten put me through these last few weeks without suddenly wanting to crush something to smithereens with my bare hands. I spot one of Jayson's plastic tape cases in the console between our seats. It'll do just fine.

"It's hard when you have to depend on someone else, especially when they're unreliable," Jay says with the voice of experience, even though he's only a year older. He spots me clutching the tape case a bit too tightly and takes it away, keeping one hand on the wheel. "So where does this leave you now? Are you going to give up this travel thing and go to Yale with me in the fall?"

"I don't know yet, *Dad*." I sigh, playing with the frayed edge of my cutoffs instead.

"I'm just asking. . . ."

"I think I'll just hang around here for a while—if that's okay."

"Take as long as you want," my brother says, looking over his left shoulder to pass. "But you should probably make your mind up quick about school. There's a lot of paperwork for incoming freshmen—"

Diversion . . . diversion . . . I need a diversion. . . .

"Jay! What happened to your hand?" I shout, pointing to the tiny white bandage taped over my brother's right palm. "Did you cut yourself?"

Jay glares at me out of the corner of his eye. "It's just a splinter I got when I picked up a two-by-four. It got infected. Don't change the subject."

I groan inwardly. Mom and Dad would be so proud if they could hear the way my brother, Mr. Responsible, was lecturing me right now. Come to think of it, he could be rambling on about the average annual rainfall in Zimbabwe and they'd be proud of that, too.

"You might as well go to college like you'd originally planned," he continues on. "I mean, you're not going to travel by yourself—"

"I don't know," I answer stubbornly. "I might."

"It's not a good idea."

I kick off my boots and peel off my damp socks, letting my toes wriggle free. Jayson discreetly opens the window a crack. "Did I mention Kirsten was disappointed when you weren't there to see me off?" I ask.

Jay knows I'm trying to change the subject again, but for some reason, this time he can't resist. "Oh, yeah?"

"She said she was looking forward to seeing her old 'lab partner' again. How come you didn't tell me you guys were friends in high school?"

Jay shrugs sheepishly. "It was just chem lab, Miranda. It didn't seem important."

"It seemed pretty important to her," I say, needling him. The edges of Jayson's ears are turning red. I'm exaggerating a bit here, just so he'll stop bugging me about school. Like most guys, the topic of women always seems to leave Jay a little flustered. "If I didn't know better, I'd think she had a crush on you."

"Nice try, Miranda." Jay stares intently on the road ahead, his ears turning a deep shade of crimson. "When we get to the apartment, remind me to show you the Yale course catalog. Maybe you'll find something you're interested in."

Or maybe not.